The

Lost Lady

A Sequel to *Tea Leaves and Tarot Cards*

JACQUELINE SEEWALD

LUMINOSITY PUBLISHING LLP

THE LOST LADY

A Sequel to *Tea Leaves and Tarot Cards*

ISBN: 978-1-7384979-3-5

Cover Art by Poppy Designs

QUOTE

“’Tis better to have loved and lost than never to have loved at all.”

—Alfred, Lord Tennyson, *In Memorium A. H. H.*

DEDICATION

This novel is dedicated to the memory of Monte Richard Seewald, a wonderful husband, who supported me in every way possible.

LONDON, 1816

CHAPTER ONE

BRIANNA WAS EXHAUSTED. Even using both hands, the carpet bag she carried became increasingly heavy—although it had not seemed so when she began her walk just after dawn. Now she felt as if she had been walking forever, most of the time lost and confused because she did not know London at all.

Arriving at a busy thoroughfare, she sighed with relief, feeling safer here. She caught the attention of a young woman strolling with a maid.

"What street is this?" Brianna asked.

The well-dressed young woman looked her up and down with disdain. "You are on Bond Street, of course. Bond Street is the most fashionable shopping area in all of London. The best dressmakers and tailors, jewelers and bootmakers, tobacconists and haberdashers all have well-appointed shops along here. I take it you are from the country."

"Yes," she replied. It was simpler to agree.

The young woman moved on, and Brianna looked around her. The street was full of large coaches. She noticed one with a crest on the door and another with gilt adornments. It hung on high springs and was drawn by four matched bay horses. Several footmen dressed in colorful livery ran beside each of the carriages. Wheels splashed in the dirt, sending up mud in black spurts. She moved carefully to avoid having her clothing ruined. What little she possessed must be protected.

Brianna did not know what she should do. Where was she to go? She could not return to Cousin Ogden. She shuddered at the thought. They had probably discovered her gone by now, Ogden and his mistress Lizette. Perhaps they would not care. She listened the previous night at their door after they thought she was asleep, believing she imbibed the drugged hot chocolate Lizette had tried to force on her. One taste and Brianna knew there was something wrong with the beverage. She waited and dumped it into the chamber pot beneath the bed and then pretended to be asleep when Lizette checked on her later.

The conversation she eavesdropped on was equal parts shocking and enlightening. It seemed they planned to leave this morning for the continent after Ogden completed selling her to a brothel owner.

"We should not have to do this," Lizette said.

"I have no choice. Would you rather I sold you to him?"

"If it wasn't for your gambling debts which left you owing a great deal of money, we would not have this problem. You spend way beyond your family allowance."

"I do not require lectures, least of all from you. Another word and I'll leave you behind as well."

Brianna had trembled with horror as she crept away. But she did not panic. She had been through worse and survived. There was nothing to do but wait for them to go to sleep, pack quickly, and then creep out of Grenville Ogden's lodgings.

Brianna did not believe her mother would have left her with such a despicable man if she realized how morally corrupt her cousin had become. But Mama had been gone from England almost as many years as Brianna had been alive. And Brianna had turned nineteen on her last birthday.

Mama had given Ogden money for taking care of Brianna but had not given any to her directly. At school, she had no need for money. Everything had been provided. After Mama stopped sending the required tuition, the sisters who ran the school in Zurich were in a quandary. Brianna was almost as frightened then as she was now. However, when she offered to work at the school, Genvieve and Denise Duvall decided it was a good idea. She'd been one of their best students. At sixteen, she was quite capable of working with the younger children. For three years, the arrangement worked well. Unfortunately, Mama finally did send a payment which the sisters returned, saying Brianna more than earned her tuition.

Mama had arrived at the girls' seminary outraged. She explained that the war had kept her from contacting them for the past few years.

"However, I am a duchess. No child of mine will work for a living. That is unacceptable, insupportable." In high dudgeon, Mama removed her from the school that had provided the only safe and stable haven she had ever known.

Mama left her in London, and here she was in her serviceable wool garment which was entirely too hot to be worn on this June day with the sun now beating down on her. She had neither eaten nor drunk anything since the previous day and was feeling faint. Brianna began to sway as dizziness and then darkness took hold of her.

CHAPTER TWO

JAMES WINTHROP WAS GROWING IMPATIENT. He tapped his foot and then consulted his pocket watch. His mother, Anna Winthrop, promised she would only be a short time in the milliner's shop. Obviously, his sense of time and hers were quite different.

Still, he could not be upset with her. Ivy, his mother's maid, had taken ill and could not shop with her this morning. He disliked being taken away from his office, but his mother rarely got out as it was. After his father's death a year ago, she had been deeply depressed. James Winthrop, Sr. had been the rock of their small family. Besides being a major industrialist and shipping magnate, he was a wonderful father and loving husband. Since James was an only child, he felt a sense of responsibility for his mother, as well as the company which was handed down and built up through many generations of Winthrops.

However, it was a decidedly warm day, and he began to perspire as he waited beside the family carriage. Neither the coachman nor footman made any complaint, but he could tell by their expressions they were as physically uncomfortable as he was.

Without warning, a young woman who appeared to be struggling with a carpetbag began to fall into a faint in front of him. If not for his quick reflexes, she would have dropped to the ground. He caught her in his arms.

"Are you all right?" he asked.

She did not answer. Her eyes were closed, her cheeks flushed. He could not help but notice that she was both pretty and young.

"Rob," he called out to his footman. "A hand here if you will." The girl, though slender, seemed to be growing heavier by the moment, a total dead weight.

"Of course, sir," Rob said as he hopped forward. He was young and well-muscled, just what James needed in this situation.

Together, they lifted the young woman and placed her inside the carriage. She still appeared to be unconscious.

"Get my mother. She is at the millinery shop up the street. Tell her she is needed immediately."

The footman left to do his bidding. James removed a handkerchief and mopped his brow. In his twenty-six years, he had never faced such an odd situation. But he was confident his mother would know what to do.

James was glad when his mother arrived. It seemed like an eternity, although in reality, it had only been a few minutes. Apparently, Rob had already informed his mother of the problem because she immediately hurried to the carriage. He helped her step inside.

"James, please reach into my reticule and remove the smelling salts."

He joined his mother on the cushy seats of the well-sprung carriage, while rummaging around in her reticule that seemed to hold something for every imaginable occasion.

"You will find the vinaigrette is a small bottle with a perforated top. It is scented with lavender," she instructed.

After his mother applied the smelling salts, James was relieved to see the young woman revive. She moaned softly as unfocused large, dark blue eyes flickered open.

"James would you please have a word with our coachman. I believe William always carries a flask of spirits," his mother said. "Perhaps you might borrow it from him? This girl requires some form of liquid. The clothing she is wearing is unsuitable, much too warm for such a day."

James was only too happy to comply. Most of all, he was grateful the young woman was alive. He'd feared she might be dead or dying.

CHAPTER THREE

Brianna was confused. Where was she? What had happened to her?

"Are you all right, my dear?" It was a woman's voice, gently solicitous.

Brianna stirred and looked at her.

"Don't be alarmed," the woman said. "You fainted and my son carried you into our coach."

Brianna was appalled. "I must apologize," she said.

"Nonsense! That you must not do. Are you feeling ill?"

Brianna shook her head and then wished she hadn't. There was still a vague dizziness. "I am sorry to have inconvenienced you so."

"Why are you out here carrying a heavy bag on the street? Are you running away from home?" A young man sitting beside the woman spoke in a sharper manner.

"No, I–I don't have a home."

"Are you an orphan then?"

Brianna was taken by his appearance. He was very handsome. Although conservatively dressed, his ruddy good looks were pleasing. She glanced from him to his mother who was a handsome woman and noted the resemblance. Wisps of dark brown hair had escaped the woman's fashionable bonnet.

"I am not precisely an orphan. You see my mother took me from my school in Switzerland and brought me here to London. She had pressing business on the continent and left me with a cousin. Unfortunately, that gentleman was in debt and leaving the country himself. Mama did not know this. She provided him with a sum of money for my support. I, unfortunately, had no money. I left quietly at dawn thinking I might locate an agency that would place me in a position. I have already been teaching at my school. But I do not know London and I became distressed. It is also much warmer here in spring than in Zurich. I am not accustomed to such heat."

"You poor girl! Of course, we wish to help you. Do you have any other relatives to whom we might take you?" the woman said.

Brianna bit her lower lip and shook her head. "There is no one."

"You would need a reference to obtain a position in any case," the handsome young man said.

"Oh, I hadn't thought of that." She was dismayed.

"Well, I propose a solution. At least for the time being, you may accept a position as my companion," the woman said. She looked to be in her middle forties, hardly a woman who required a companion.

The young man's dark brown eyes opened wide in surprise. He placed his hand on his mother's arm as if to restrain her. "Mother, I think we must talk about this matter privately."

The lady shook her head. "It is not necessary." She turned to Brianna. "I am Anna Winthrop. This is my son James. And who are you?"

"Just… Brianna." Her voice sounded like rust; her throat was terribly dry.

"Well, just Brianna, I believe we will rub well together." Mrs. Winthrop turned to her son. "James, I know you are questioning my decision, but I believe it is a good one. In any case, you will not dissuade me. Brianna is in need of a position. I intend to provide one."

"Perhaps we might discuss this later," James suggested.

Mrs. Winthrop shook her head. "The matter is settled."

Brianna hardly knew what to think.

James Winthrop eyed her with suspicion. Clearly, he did not trust her. Brianna conceded she would probably have felt the same under similar circumstances. She did not fault him for being protective of his mother.

"Let us proceed to Gunter's. I feel a desire for their splendid ices." Mrs. Winthrop appeared to be in a cheerful mood.

"Mother, I should be taking you home and returning to the office."

"James, you are in charge there. No one will question you for returning a bit later than expected."

"Very well," James responded with a disapproving frown. He called up to the coachman. "Take us to Gunter's Tea Shop."

CHAPTER FOUR

James kept a tight lid on his opinion of his mother's strange behavior which was so uncharacteristic of her. Anna Winthrop was reclusive if anything. She did not socialize with many people. The love of her life had always been his father. She never talked about her family, of whom he knew nothing. She rarely went out. He loved his mother dearly, but she was not easy to understand.

Their coach took them to Gunter's located at No. 7–8 Berkeley Square in London's West End. It was a popular and busy establishment, particularly at this time of year.

"Such a splendid place," his mother said to the young girl. "They have ice cream, mousse, and sorbet as well as ices." She pointed to the menu. "And note all the flavors. Why there is maple, bergamot, pineapple, pistachio, jasmine, white coffee, chocolate, vanilla, elderflower, parmesan, and lavender. I hardly know what to order."

"I believe a dish of vanilla will be sufficient for me," James said, becoming increasingly annoyed by his mother's peculiar behavior.

"What will you have, Brianna?" his mother asked.

"The vanilla will be fine for me as well. Thank you."

"Well, I must be more adventurous. I have learned that life is too short. One must indulge in some adventures. I believe pineapple will suit me."

When their order arrived, they ate in relative silence, except for his mother stating how good her choice had been. He rarely remembered her in better spirits. It was puzzling.

As they rose to leave the shop, his mother pointed across the street. "Look at the young people over there eating their ices in the park under the maple trees. Perhaps we should have done the same."

"We would only have attracted bees," he said.

His mother sighed. "Sometimes, you are too sensible, but then so am I."

"Usually, but not today," he said, glancing at the young girl who stood beside his mother, eyes shyly downcast.

He dropped them both at the family home in Belgravia and proceeded to his office almost in a daze. The girl named Brianna—no last name given—was beautiful and well-spoken. He would not deny that he found her extremely attractive. But who was she? Her story was at best vague in detail. The fact that his mother had immediately taken to the girl was as mysterious as the girl herself. However, he had no more time to dwell on the matter. He resolved he would talk to both again this evening. Perhaps by then his mother would behave more sensibly. For now, he must concentrate on the work at hand. Many people's livelihoods depended upon him. His father entrusted him with work of great importance. He had been trained from childhood, schooled at home by the best of tutors, and taken into business to learn from his father from an early age. Still, he admitted the events of this morning continued to trouble him.

CHAPTER FIVE

BRIANNA LOOKED AROUND HER IN surprise. The house she had entered was elegant and tastefully furnished. It was one of wealth. Mrs. Winthrop was greeted by servants in the foyer. She introduced Brianna and told both the butler and housekeeper that Brianna had been hired as a companion, and she was to be given a room near that of Mrs. Winthrop. The servants were polite and did not ask questions. Brianna gathered Mrs. Winthrop did not have close relationships with her servants. The kindness and warmth the woman had shown her were not accorded the butler or housekeeper. Anna Winthrop's manner with them was formal and somewhat brusque. It surprised Brianna.

She followed the middle-aged housekeeper to a clean, neat room upstairs. A young maid soon appeared. She brought a basin of water, wash cloth and towel to Brianna and placed them on a nightstand and then proceeded to unpack her belongings, putting them into a cherry wood bureau. Brianna turned to her.

"Have you worked here long?" she asked.

The girl, who was clearly only a few years younger than herself, looked embarrassed. "This is my first proper job, Miss. Usually, I dust and clean downstairs. But Mrs. Dunne, the housekeeper, she thought you'd be needing a maid seeing as you didn't arrive with one." Brianna detected the slightest Irish lilt in the maid's accent which seemed a match for her green eyes and red hair.

"I do not usually have a maid. I have managed for myself." She had earned her tuition for some years by being helpful in every way expected of her. When the duties of a maid were in short supply, Brianna was more than willing to do her part.

The girl seemed agitated. "Oh, please, I really want this job. Don't send me off."

"What? No," she assured the maid. "I could use help learning about this household."

The girl smiled, her expression no longer guarded but warm and friendly. "I can do that and more. I'm Gwen, and it's happy I am to serve you."

"I am Brianna, and I am not used to being served, but I will appreciate your help as I have said. After all, I am a stranger in a strange land. Do you like working here, Gwen?"

"Oh, yes, I do. The missus and her son are very nice people and not demanding at all. Not stuck up either. Of course, Mrs. Dunne is most particular and so is the butler." The girl sniffed her distaste for the senior servants.

"I would like to rest for a while," Brianna said, politely dismissing Gwen.

"Oh, yes, of course. I will be back later to let you know when Mrs. Winthrop expects you for tea." With that, the girl left her, and Brianna breathed a sigh of relief.

She needed to be alone to gather her thoughts and emotions. Mrs. Winthrop's generosity toward her was unexpected but appreciated. She was not going to question it. Brianna was grateful. James Winthrop had been suspicious of her, with good reason, she admitted. But she was not about to tell either mother or son all the details of her life. She would probably have shocked them. No, that would not do at all.

CHAPTER SIX

AFTER A LONG DAY OF meetings and conferences with business associates, James arrived home tired and hungry. He looked forward to an early dinner and reading a book in the library. He and his mother often read companionably together in the evenings. He preferred nonfiction, biographies, and histories, while his mother loved novels. Her favorites were romance fiction. Occasionally, he teased her about it.

As he entered the drawing room on the main floor, he heard music being played. Someone was making use of the pianoforte. He thought it must be his mother. She had stopped playing after his father died. He smiled and hoped she was coming out of the deep mourning she had felt during that terrible time. But it turned out not to be his mother sitting at the piano but Brianna.

The girl began singing in a language he did not know. He realized it was German sounding. Her voice was a sweet soprano, angelic and pleasing. When she caught sight of him, she stopped singing. She rose to her feet as did his mother.

"Please do not stop. That was quite pleasant," he assured her.

Brianna's face flushed. He felt fully aware of her, observing that her face was heart-shaped. She was taller than his mother, with a slender, willowy body. Her eyes were large and liquid, a dark blue-violet in color, her hair a honey blond.

"Do you sing songs in many languages?" he inquired.

She nodded. "In Switzerland, there is an international population. At school, I studied French and German as well as English. In travels with my mother, I became familiar with some Italian and Spanish as well."

"James, Brianna and I had an interesting chat over tea. She has taught music among other things." His mother seemed animated.

"Perhaps, if she stays, she will encourage you to play the piano again too."

"I am still in mourning. It would not be appropriate."

James frowned. "Mother, it is now over a year. Father would not want you to continue to grieve so." He pointed to her black dress. "That is not your best color."

Brianna moved away from the piano bench. "Your son is correct, Mrs. Winthrop. You were cheerful this morning. You must be so again. Perhaps some lavender gowns would suit or even light gray."

"I don't know," Mrs. Winthrop said.

"Mother, you must leave off the black bombazine and crape."

Anna Winthrop shrugged. "Perhaps," she said diffidently.

"It is this house," James said. "We should make it more pleasant as it was before Father passed. Then you will feel better."

"I will gladly help," Brianna said, her manner earnest.

His mother smiled. He conceded that this young woman was having a good influence on his mother. Perhaps she had seen something in the girl beyond her good looks. But who was this girl really? They knew nothing about her, and he found that disturbing. He had arrived home with the intention of convincing his mother that hiring an unknown person was a mistake, that she must allow him to discharge her, but now he was not as certain.

In the next few weeks that followed, James started to see even more dramatic changes in his mother's behavior. She began going out regularly with Brianna at her side. Lavender silk was selected for new frocks from the modiste.

Several times he managed to come home for nuncheon and found his mother out in the garden with Brianna, both of them sitting at easels and painting with watercolors. It seemed Brianna had sketched garden scenes for them to paint. Another day they were embroidering pillowcases. In fact, each day, it appeared, Brianna was filling his mother's time with activities she could enjoy.

One evening after a particularly stressful day, James found himself unable to get to sleep. He went downstairs to the library to select a book. Reading usually relaxed him. As he entered the library, he saw Brianna sitting by candlelight and reading.

"We seem to have had the same idea," he said.

She jumped up startled. "I should go," she said.

"No, please stay. Enjoy your book."

"It is one your mother chose. I like it exceedingly."

"A romance I suppose?"

"A novel entitled *Persuasion*. It is very popular."

"My mother appears much happier since you have come here. You seem to be helping her. You brought her back to life."

Brianna's face flushed from the praise. "Thank you. But I owe you both a great deal. You saved my life. I will always be grateful. And I do enjoy being with your mother. She is a delightful person."

"She seems to feel the same way about you," James observed.

He wondered if she realized the way she modestly lowered her eyes made her especially appealing.

"Have you decided to approve of me?" The dark blue orbs fixed on him with unexpected intensity.

"It was never a question of that."

She turned away from him. "I realize I shared little about my past with you."

"Who are you really, Brianna?"

She folded her hands together. "We all need to keep our secrets."

"You are indeed a woman of mystery. Innocent yet knowing."

He moved closer to her. She backed away.

"There is not much to tell." She sounded uneasy.

"I think there must be. You are a puzzle, an enigma."

She shrugged. James moved even closer. He touched a lock of her honey-blond hair, moving it back from her face. Then he pulled her into his arms and kissed her. His lips were gentle at first, but when she responded, he pulled her against his body and deepened the kiss. She smelled of roses. Her lips were soft, her body pliant. He felt desire nearly overwhelm him.

Suddenly, he became aware of what he was doing and immediately released her. "I apologize," he said. "I should not have behaved in such a boorish manner. It was wrong of me. I have no intention of taking advantage of you."

James hurried out of the library as if chased by a demon and ran up the stairs without looking back. Why had he done that? How had he let himself be overcome, carried away by lust in that way? It was unacceptable.

The girl was forbidden fruit which he supposed made her a formidable temptation. Did she realize it? Was she playing some kind of game at his expense or was he merely looking for an excuse to justify his appalling behavior? Nevertheless, he must guard against the enemy within himself.

He spent a sleepless night restlessly turning and tossing in his bed.

CHAPTER SEVEN

Brianna had been enjoying her time spent with Anna Winthrop. Her employer made Brianna feel welcome from the start. They truly appreciated each other's company. The one concern she had was whether James Winthrop would accept her presence in his home. She had been aware he remained suspicious of her and kept his distance until this evening. She understood it was not personal. His motive was clearly that he wished to protect his mother.

But then he kissed her. She could scarcely believe it! The realization shocked her. Brianna admitted she greatly enjoyed that kiss. He was a very attractive man after all. Did he find her desirable? Perhaps—was it possible? Still, she knew nothing of men and how they thought, but she did read books. She realized the kiss had been inappropriate.

And then there was her mother. The duchess had many protectors over the years. She traveled constantly, restlessly, but did not remarry—could not remarry since the duke was still alive in England. Mama never discussed such matters with Brianna, but she knew. Oh God, she knew! Brianna shuddered at memories she wished to forget.

James kissing her was a complication. Brianna wished to stay in the household as Anna Winthrop's companion. It was pleasant working here, just as it had been at her school. The difference was she only had to deal with one person rather than a number of children. Anna was never difficult, just the opposite. And she was earning money for the first time. It gave Brianna a sense of self-worth and independence which she never had before in her life. It was a good feeling. She carefully saved her salary knowing that it was a source of freedom should she lose her position here.

What if Anna learned of James kissing her? Would her employer's attitude toward her change? Mama moved from one man to another. Brianna did not intend to be any man's mistress. Now that the old duke was dead, Mama intended to marry again. That was why the hurry to settle Brianna with her cousin Ogden after the new duke refused to accept Brianna. When she recalled that day, the horror of that rejection, Brianna felt the shame of it all over again. But no, she must put it out of her mind.

Sleep did not come easily that night, and when it finally did, she dreamt of a man kissing her with great passion and herself succumbing.

CHAPTER EIGHT

JAMES FOUND IT DIFFICULT TO concentrate on work the following day. His thoughts kept returning to Brianna and the kiss they shared the evening before. He never lied to himself. He would not do so now. He wanted her. He desired her. He punched his fist against the wall. He was not going to have her. It was not ethical since he had no intention of marrying the girl. In fact, he had no intention of marrying any woman ever.

He'd made a vow to himself regarding that when his father's doctor explained the nature of the illness that was slowly destroying a fine man. His father never talked about it, except to be reassuring. Out of deference to his parents, James never discussed the matter with either of them. It was too painful.

But Dr. Henderson had taken him aside and explained matters in his no-nonsense way so that James would know what to expect. "You might as well be aware, my boy, that what your father is suffering from exists in his family line."

"You mean that it's hereditary?" James asked, swallowing hard.

Dr. Henderson nodded gravely. "Not everyone must inherit it, but it seems to run in certain families. Your father began showing mild symptoms in his forties. Now at fifty, the illness is progressing at an alarming rate. As you have seen, there is some abnormality walking, involuntary movements, problems with coordination, loss of muscle, slowness in activity, increased difficulty thinking and understanding." The doctor cast his eyes downward. "It means early death."

James had been appalled. As his father's son, would this happen to him as well? No, he would not discuss the matter with his mother. In his estimation, she was too fragile. However, he decided then and there never to marry, never to have children of his own. Somehow, all the family wealth seemed to matter very little when one contemplated such harsh realities.

What of Brianna? It was best if he kept his distance. He sensed the attraction was mutual by the way she had enthusiastically responded to his kiss. But he resolved that must never happen again.

CHAPTER NINE

BRIANNA WAS IN A GOOD mood. She and Mrs. Winthrop were to go to Madame Renault's shop today.

"I have decided that you and James are right about my wardrobe. It is time I wore some more fashionable clothes. Perhaps some summer pastels. And you must have some new frocks as well, my dear. You have so little."

Brianna shook her head. "I cannot afford it as yet." Madam Renault's establishment catered to the *ton* and the most affluent ladies of the middle class. She knew Mrs. Winthrop meant well but Brianna doubted she would ever be able to shop in such an establishment for herself.

"Nonsense, I won't have my companion continue dressing as a schoolgirl in dowdy gray uniforms. I should have seen to this much earlier. I have wallowed too long in personal grief I collect. It is a form of selfishness, I fear. Come, my dear, our carriage awaits."

Anna Winthrop looked vital today. She told stories about James as a child which were endearing and amusing. Brianna noted her employer did not talk about her own life prior to her marriage. She had come to understand that Mrs. Winthrop, like herself, must have suffered in some way and did not wish to revisit those times. As she said to James, everyone had their secrets, things they did not wish to share with others.

Madame Renault had an amazing variety of gowns in all sorts of colors, fabrics, and designs, all in the current high-waisted empire fashion.

"What splendid workmanship," Mrs. Winthrop said, reverently running her fingers over a red velvet evening gown.

"This would be perfect with your coloring," the shop girl exclaimed.

"I don't go out in the evenings," Anna Winthrop said.

"Perhaps day dresses then?"

Anna nodded.

The young girl had sharp features; her narrowed eyes concentrated on Mrs. Winthrop since it was obvious that Brianna was no one of real consequence. Brianna took notice of her surroundings. She had never been in a shop like this before. There were a number of fashionables, clearly wealthy ladies discussing their orders with other shop girls. Apparently, clothing would be made-to-order after taking their measurements.

"Brianna!" She turned and was greeted with the warmest of hugs. "It is you! My dear, we looked everywhere for you. Adam had Bow Street Runners searching. We thought your mother must have taken you back to the continent with her after all."

Brianna was startled. She was uncertain how she should respond.

Mrs. Winthrop looked from Brianna to the woman who had spoken. "Brianna, please introduce me to your friend."

"Let us not stand on ceremony. I am Maeve."

Brianna realized an explanation was necessary. "Maeve is the wife of the Duke of Clarmont."

"Your Grace," Mrs. Winthrop said with a curtsey.

"Oh, no need for such formalities. Brianna is my sister-in-law after all."

Mrs. Winthrop's mouth hung open. "I–I do not understand."

Maeve looked from Brianna to Mrs. Winthrop. "I see explanations are required. I must be fitted for some sacque dresses I have ordered and then we can have tea together. As you can see, I am increasing and need a fitting." Maeve pointed to her rounding middle.

All thoughts of further shopping on this day were forgotten. By agreement, they met at Gunter's Tea Shop. Maeve had already been seated by the time they arrived. Brianna thought her sister-in-law looked radiant. Her thick, raven hair had a luster. Her silvery eyes displayed a fey quality that seemed to dissolve into mist while her skin was unusual, a deep color like fine wine. Mama had called Maeve a gypsy. Perhaps Maeve was, but Brianna did not know or care. Maeve was a striking woman with much warmth and personal magnetism. Brianna knew that if it had been up to Maeve, she would not have been forced to leave the ducal residence that awful day after the old duke's funeral. Mama had been in high dudgeon that afternoon. So had her son, the new duke. They had argued, quarreled, and said terrible things to each other. Brianna shuddered at the memory of it.

"We must all have tea and cakes," Maeve said.

They spoke little until the order was given. Maeve insisted on ordering seed cakes, crumpets, and Sally Lunn buns besides green tea.

"That is so much!' Mrs. Winthrop exclaimed.

"But we must celebrate," Maeve explained. "You see, we have searched desperately to find Brianna these many weeks. And now she is found."

Brianna was astonished. "But, Your Grace…"

"Maeve if you please." She placed her hand on Brianna's.

"His Grace would not countenance me."

Maeve frowned. "I have not forgotten, but I have forgiven. I begged him to go after you, but he was too upset after the confrontation with his mother. Brianna, you understand why he has such strong feelings toward her?"

Mrs. Winthrop looked from Maeve to Brianna with curiosity and some confusion. Brianna swallowed hard, casting her eyes downward on the tablecloth with embarrassment.

"We will not talk further of this matter here in such a public place," Maeve said. She turned to Mrs. Winthrop, and reaching into her reticule, handed the lady her card. "Is it possible for you and Brianna to come to tea tomorrow at four o'clock? We can discuss matters privately then."

Mrs. Winthrop readily agreed. Brianna did not speak. Although the tea and pastries were likely delightful, to Brianna they tasted like sawdust.

CHAPTER TEN

"BRIANNA, WHY DID YOU NOT tell us about your connection?" Mrs. Winthrop inquired on the short trip back to her home.

Brianna was removing her bonnet. She shrugged uneasily. "It does not signify."

For the first time since knowing her, Mrs. Winthrop appeared angry. Her lower lip curled. Her hands were on her hips. "I am disappointed in you. James was displeased by my hiring you with no reference to offer and giving no last name, but I stood solidly behind you. Now it seems you have been deceitful and are untrustworthy. I feel like a fool."

Brianna was appalled. "Please do not be out of countenance with me. The situation was too painful for me to discuss."

"Very well. However, I must confer with my son about this."

"Yes, I understand. But can you not wait until we speak with Maeve tomorrow? Please?"

Mrs. Winthrop hesitated. "I suppose so. Right now, I have the headache and feel I must rest for a while."

When Mrs. Winthrop left her in the hall to go upstairs, Brianna breathed a sigh of relief. Her reprieve would only be temporary, but it would give her time to think and consider what she must do and say.

~♥~

When James arrived home that evening, he was not greeted by his mother, which was unusual. No sign of Brianna either. The butler was solicitous and took his hat and coat.

"Is my mother in the library?" he asked.

"No, sir, she is resting at present. She mentioned not feeling up to snuff."

James did not like the sound of that. Since Brianna was with her, Mother had not once complained about feeling ill. He wanted to find out what was wrong but did not wish to disturb his mother if she were sleeping. Still, he found the matter troubling.

"Where is Brianna?"

"I believe the young lady is also in her own room, sir."

"Thank you, Norris."

The butler nodded. "Will that be all, sir?"

"Yes, thank you." Norris was really his father's butler, a very proper older man. He was discreet and always knew a lot more than he shared.

James decided to go to his study and read the newspapers. There was no point worrying about Mother. He would talk to her at dinner.

As it turned out, he did not have to wait that long. His mother joined him an hour before dinner. She sat down opposite him. Her brow was raised, and she was wringing her hands. These were not good signs.

"James, I want to discuss a matter that is troubling me. I would appreciate your advice."

He put away his reading materials. "Of course, Mother. What do you wish to discuss?"

She lowered her gaze. "It concerns Brianna."

"Ah," he said and waited. Had Mother found out something displeasing about the girl? Was she thinking of letting Brianna go? He would not have been surprised. It would likely be for the best. The girl was too much of a temptation for him.

His mother cleared her throat. "For some time, I thought Brianna might be the bi-blow of a wealthy family. If she were born on the wrong side of the blanket, so to speak, I would understand, of course."

"Yes, I rather thought the same thing," he said, "since she did not provide us with a last name."

"As enlightened people, I did not hold it against the girl. Of course, lovely as she is, I would not consider her an appropriate match for you. The Winthrop family is distinguished after all."

"Mother, I am not thinking of marrying."

"Well, of course, not to anyone inappropriate."

James shook his head. He almost told his mother the reason he did not intend to ever marry but realized that would only upset her further.

"What is it about Brianna that is troubling you?"

His mother licked dry lips. "We were at Madam Renault's shop today. A lady came up to Brianna. She claimed to have been searching for the girl for weeks."

"Really? That is surprising." James went to the credenza against the wall and reached for the brandy decanter kept there. He poured a small amount into a crystal snifter for his mother and another for himself. He sensed whatever she had to tell him would prove shocking.

"The lady in question turned out to be the Duchess of Clarmont. Her Grace is Maeve de Villers. She claims to be the sister-in-law of Brianna. She invited us to tea tomorrow afternoon at the ducal residence."

"This sounds very odd indeed," James said, sipping his brandy thoughtfully.

"What do you make of this, James? Should I go?"

"Would you like me to join you and Brianna?"

"I think it might be wise. I find the situation most disturbing."

"Of course. I shall reschedule some appointments and we will go together. I do not suppose Brianna offered you an explanation?"

His mother shook her head. "No, but she didn't deny what the lady said either."

"Perhaps at last we will find out who exactly Brianna is tomorrow." He finished his brandy and then reached over to pour himself another.

CHAPTER ELEVEN

Brianna hardly slept that night. In the morning, bleary-eyed, she went downstairs for a bracing cup of coffee. She took eggs and ham from the sideboard but found she had no appetite to eat them.

"Has Mrs. Winthrop been down for breakfast?" she asked the maid who served her beverage.

"No, ma'am. The Mrs. is having breakfast sent to her room. I don't think she wishes to be disturbed."

How awful! Mrs. Winthrop was clearly out of countenance with her. Brianna wished to explain matters, but what should she say? It was so difficult. Perhaps it would be best to speak in front of Maeve and sort things out. But the thought her brother might be present as well was deeply troubling.

The hours passed slowly. Mrs. Winthrop did not come downstairs until it was time to leave. She spoke not a single word to Brianna in the carriage. When Brianna attempted to converse with her employer, Anna turned away. Brianna had a sinking feeling. This was not going well.

The ducal townhouse on Curzon Street was impressive. The building had a pastel-colored stucco façade with ornate wrought-iron detailing on the balconies and porches, colonnaded walkways, curved windows and front doorways, rooftop balustrades, wooden window shutters, and classical friezes. A footman dressed in livery opened the door for them and led them past an imposing central staircase. A butler greeted them, and they followed him into an elegant drawing room with a large carved marble fireplace and hand-painted silk wallpaper. The main color was azure blue.

"Her Grace will be with you presently," the elderly butler informed them.

Mrs. Winthrop seated herself on a settee while Brianna looked out the front window. It seemed as if they waited forever but Maeve joined them several minutes later.

"Brianna, won't you sit down? I shall ring for tea now if that meets with your approval," Maeve said turning to Mrs. Winthrop.

"Thank you, Your Grace," Mrs. Winthrop said politely.

No words were exchanged until Maeve had poured tea from a sterling silver service into fine China cups and offered small cakes and sandwiches on a silver tray. Brianna only took a few sips of her tea.

Maeve turned to Brianna. "I must ask how you came to be living with the Winthrops."

Brianna told Maeve what had transpired. "Grenville Ogden is a terrible person," she concluded. "I am certain Mama did not realize it, but she was in a hurry to leave for Italy. She planned to remarry now that she was widowed."

"She could have taken you with her," Maeve said frowning.

Brianna bit her lower lip. "Mama has always been somewhat vain about her appearance. I do not think she told her fiancé her real age. In fact, I do not believe he knew I existed. Likely, she feared he would not marry her if he were aware."

Maeve shook her head in disgust. "Do not make excuses for her. I am confused as to her reason for bringing you to London, knowing there would not be a welcome here."

"She removed me from my school when she learned I was teaching there. In her mind, it was beneath a lady to labor."

"I disagree," Maeve said. "However, your mother was from a very different background than mine."

"But why did you not tell us who you were?" Mrs. Winthrop cast an accusing look in Brianna's direction.

"I was too ashamed. I did not think my brother would allow me to live here under any circumstances. He told my mother we were to leave when she brought me here that awful day."

Maeve came to Brianna and took her hand. "My dear, it was just after his father's funeral." Maeve cast her long-lashed silver eyes downward. "He had been drinking. He was not himself. He was in his cups. Your mother simply chose the wrong time to approach him."

"But, Maeve, he said such terrible things!"

"Yes, and so did your mother. You were not yet born when the incident they spoke of occurred, and your brother was himself then a child."

"What incident?" Mrs. Winthrop asked.

"I do not know all the details," Maeve quickly said.

Brianna was grateful for Maeve's unwillingness to gossip. She was spared further embarrassment by the arrival of James Winthrop. The butler announced him. Maeve rose and James entered the room, bowing to Maeve. They exchanged pleasantries.

"I was held up at the office but sent word that I would come here directly. I hope that is not too much of an inconvenience," he said to Maeve.

Brianna thought how handsome he looked, tall and well-dressed. He accepted tea from Maeve and joined his mother on the settee. Briana seated herself on a straight-back chair with gilt embroidery.

Before more words could be exchanged the Duke of Clarmont entered the room. Brianna considered him a most imposing figure. The light caught the gold hi-lights of his fashionably cut hair.

"Maeve, my love, please introduce me to these people."

"Adam, your sister is here with the Winthrops who have provided care for her when we could not do so."

The duke nodded, "Madam, Mr. Winthop, we appreciate your kindness. And now you have brought my sister here. We welcome you into our home." His voice, deep, rich, and cultured, could have charmed a cobra. But his face was hard, jaded, and knowing.

"We would like to continue to employ Brianna if allowed," Mrs. Winthrop said. "She has proven to be a wonderful companion. After my husband's death, I felt only deep sorrow. Brianna has been able to help me overcome my grief to some degree."

"I assure you I am glad to hear this," the duke said.

"Actually, the Winthrops saved my life. I do not know what would have become of me if they had not taken me in. It is I who owe them." Brianna smiled at Anna and James. "They have been kindness itself."

"Yes, all well and good," the duke tapped his long-tapered fingers against the marble fireplace mantle in an impatient manner. "However, you do understand that you are the sister of a duke and that commands a certain place in society. You cannot continue working in some lowly position."

Brianna was suddenly very angry. "As I understand it, you told my mother I was nothing but a half-sister, her illegitimate child at that. That was why I was thrown out along with her that horrible day. No, do not bother to deny it. Maeve and I were outside your study. The door was partially open, your voices were raised, and we heard every word."

"Must we speak of such matters in front of strangers?"

"Mama took me from my school where I was quite happy teaching the children. Now you would do the same and remove me from a position I enjoy. That is not just!"

"You are not of age. You will do as I say. You belong here with us. There is nothing further to say." He practically snarled at her.

Brianna burst into tears. Maeve came and held her. "We have a lovely room prepared for you, my dear. All will be well, and you may see the Winthrops as often as you like."

Anna took her hand. "Yes, Her Grace is right, my dear, all will be well. You will see." Brianna observed there were tears in Mrs. Winthrop's eyes too.

"We wish only the best for you," James said. His fond gaze moved over her as if memorizing her features.

When they had gone, Brianna felt bereft. "How could you?" she said, pointing an accusing finger at her brother.

He narrowed his indigo eyes. "Anyone would be grateful for what we can offer you." He shook his head. "You are your mother's daughter. Nothing ever satisfied her either."

CHAPTER TWELVE

JAMES DID HIS BEST TO comfort his mother in their coach on the drive home, but she was inconsolable.

"I knew as soon as we met Her Grace that everything was about to change. I believe Brianna thought I was rejecting her but that was not the case at all. She should have told us, James, so I would not have grown so attached to her. For me, this is a dreadful loss. I feel betrayed."

He held his mother to him. "I understand," he said. The truth was he felt much the same way. He hadn't wished to admit to himself how he felt about Brianna. Under different circumstances, he would have offered for her. But he felt just as strongly as ever that it would be wrong of him to marry any woman, even Brianna. Ironically, when she worked as a companion to his mother, Brianna would have been considered too lowly for a man of his means to marry. Now, finding out her brother was a duke made her a touch above his station in life. Aristocrats married their own in large measure. They looked down on the bourgeoisie. Even the illegitimate children of the ton were given opportunities that people of his class did not have.

James brought his mother home and went back to his office. He was not in a good mood. He wished Brianna had never come into their lives.

~♥~

MAEVE LED BRIANNA to the room that would be hers. It was large and elegant.

A fine bed with a beautiful floral comforter was the centerpiece. There was a gold-framed mirror, truly a work of art, hanging on one wall. Damask wallpaper was detailed in a rose pattern. It was far more beautiful than anything she had ever known in her life, and yet she could not feel content.

"This will be like sleeping in a garden," Brianna said.

"I do hope you like it." Maeve smiled warmly at her.

"You are very kind."

"But you are not happy to be here," Maeve said.

Brianna shook her head. "I simply wish I could have stayed with the Winthrops."

Maeve sat down on the bed and Brianna joined her.

"I do understand," Maeve said, "but you belong here with your family."

"With a brother who at best dislikes me?"

Maeve frowned. "It is not that precisely. How much were you told about the events occurring before your birth?"

"Nothing much really. However, when Mama first brought me to my school, I overheard a woman, the wife of a diplomat who was registering her daughter as well. She appeared to know who my mother was and gave her the cut direct. Mama raised her chin as if the woman was vermin beneath contempt and walked away. Then that same woman turned to my teachers. 'Do you know who that woman is?' she asked in an outraged tone of voice, pointing to Mama. 'She is the Duchess of Clarmont,' Madam Genvieve replied. My teacher put an emphasis on the word Duchess. The other lady clearly took umbrage. 'She is no better than a common slut, and her bastard child should not be admitted here. I have changed my mind. My daughter will not be attending your school since you have no discernment as to applicants.' With that, she left in a huff. I was crushed. I did not know the whole story, of course, and did not try to ask."

Maeve viewed her sympathetically. "Not everyone is like that woman."

"I daresay I hope not."

"Why don't you rest until dinner? You must be tired."

Brianna nodded. "I am weary. Thank you for being so understanding."

Maeve rose to leave. Brianna thought her sister-in-law radiated serene energy. She lay down on top of the comforter and closed her eyes. She must have slept for a time because she was jolted awake by someone calling her name.

Brianna sat upright and rubbed her eyes.

"Oh, I'm sorry Miss, didn't mean to disturb you, but I brought your things. Mrs. Winthrop thought you'd be needing them."

"Gwen, I am glad you are here," Brianna said to the young maid.

"Do you want me to stay on? Mrs. Winthrop thought you might."

"Yes, I do want that." Anna Winthrop was so kind and thoughtful.

Gwen helped her change into her light gray frock. It was plain, not good enough for the home of a duke, but it would have to do for the time being. She went downstairs not quite certain when she was expected for dinner. Brianna visited the drawing room they frequented earlier. No one else was present. Perhaps she had come down too early. She consulted the ornate ormolu clock on the marble mantle. It was seven p.m. That was dinner hour at the Winthrops. Perhaps the duke kept more fashionable hours. She would soon find out.

Fifteen minutes passed before Maeve joined her. "Let us go to the dining room," she said, "Adam will be joining us directly."

They were seated by the time the duke entered the room. Brianna suddenly felt nervous. When the first course was placed in front of her, she found herself unable to lift a spoon.

"Don't you like turtle soup?" Maeve asked. "Perhaps you would prefer something else?"

Brianna shook her head. "I have little appetite."

"I am sorry to hear that," Maeve said.

"Do not coddle the girl," the duke said, sounding annoyed.

"Perhaps we should talk and clear the air so to speak," Maeve said. "I believe you owe Bri an apology."

The duke narrowed his indigo eyes. "I never apologize, and there is no need now. Also, my dear, do not refer to the girl as Bri as if she were a Frenchy cheese."

Brianna was surprised that Maeve did not take offense. She seemed unperturbed.

"Still, there are some things that must be discussed."

"After dinner so that it does not interfere with our digestion."

Eight courses were served in all. After the soup came pheasant, venison, lobster patties, and oysters. For dessert there was a variety of fruits and pastries, all served with both white and red wine. Brianna sat quietly and ate little. Finally, to her relief, the meal ended.

"Now may we speak?" Maeve insisted.

"Of course, my darling wife." The duke stood and kissed Maeve on the forehead.

By agreement, they went to the drawing room and the duke shut the doors.

"What exactly do you wish to discuss?" the duke asked his wife.

"What caused your anger toward your mother? Why exactly did you ask her to leave the house and take Brianna with her?"

The duke let out a deep sigh. "It is all best forgotten."

"It is not only Maeve who particularly wishes to know, but myself," Brianna said.

"It is a nasty business, as I have said best forgotten, but I suppose neither of you will let the matter rest until you have all the information." He sat down heavily beside Maeve on the gilt settee.

"Where to begin? As a child, I adored my mother. She was young when she had me. Married at seventeen right out of the schoolroom, scooped up by the duke my father. She was a great beauty, a diamond of the first water, much admired. My father was much older. His first wife died in childbirth without providing him with an heir.

"He was delighted when I was born. However, as I understand it, the marriage did not go well after that. My mother, being young, wanted to attend parties and balls. Unfortunately, my father enjoyed drinking with his male friends. He quite preferred their company. Mother felt neglected. She attended gatherings without him. She basked in the admiration of other men. When I was nine years of age, she took a lover."

"Do you know that for certain?" Maeve asked.

The duke nodded. "Unfortunately, I do. You see Mother did the unpardonable in ton society. She was indiscreet. She was caught with her lover in her bedchamber by none other than my father. He may have been in his cups, but nonetheless, he called the fellow out. There was a duel. Pistols were chosen. My father shot the younger man dead, right through the heart

I was told by his cousin the Duke of Rundwall who acted as his second. Sadly, my father received a head wound that left him in a vegetative state for the rest of his life. You can imagine what a terrible scandal the matter became. It shamed all of us."

"But Mama especially," Brianna surmised.

"She deserved it. Then to add insult to injury, you were born not long after."

"And that was when Mama decided to leave the country." Brianna understood a great deal more now. "I suppose everyone in society turned their backs on her."

The duke nodded his agreement. "Even her own relatives were ashamed of her."

"At least you were cared for by your mother," Maeve said to Brianna. "There are those who do not keep children of questionable paternity."

"I suppose you are right," Brianna agreed. Deep down she always thought her mother disliked her. Brianna never could do anything that pleased Mama. Perhaps there was a certain amount of resentment that she had ever been born.

Brianna left her brother and Maeve. She had a great deal to think about. She spent another night sleeping poorly with vivid nightmares rousing her at dawn.

CHAPTER THIRTEEN

IN THE WEEKS THAT FOLLOWED, James watched his mother withdraw again. It was painful to observe. If only things had worked out with Brianna. Ironically, the girl was now a touch above them. As the sister of an aristocrat, a duke at that, she must be in a different social sphere.

He took time away from his business one afternoon to escort his mother to the Minerva Press circulating library which had become fashionable. Many ladies had subscriptions there including his mother.

Who should they see but Brianna. Despite common sense, he felt his heart beating faster. She looked different, dressed in white muslin, flounced and ruffled. She wore a buff-colored, chip straw bonnet with a band of white rosebuds around the rim and looked beautiful. She held several books in her gloved hands.

When she looked up and saw them, Brianna smiled warmly. "How good it is to see you both! I have thought of you often these past weeks."

"You are in looks," James said. He saw her blush and regretted his compliment.

"James is quite right," his mother said.

Brianna reached out her hand to Mrs. Winthrop. "I will invite you to tea soon again."

"Perhaps, you should not," James cautioned.

Brianna frowned. "Why ever not?"

"I believe your brother would disapprove," James said.

"But you are both dear to me."

His mother squeezed his arm. "Of course, we will come if invited."

"Good, then it is settled. I must leave now but will send an invitation soon."

After Brianna had gone, his mother turned to him with an inquiring look.

"What is wrong? Why are you opposed to spending time with Brianna?"

James looked about. This was a place where women often came to socialize and exchange gossip. Fortunately, no one was nearby to overhear their conversation.

"Brianna is not of our class, Mother. Such a visit would prove awkward at best."

His mother glared at him. "Her Grace has shown us nothing but kindness. She puts on no airs of any kind. As for Brianna, she is a sweet, gentle girl who has not had an easy life. She is no spoiled, selfish aristocrat."

"But what of the duke? Trust me, we will not be welcome in his mansion."

"We will see," his mother said in a mulish tone of voice while raising her chin.

He let out a deep sigh. She was not going to be easy to convince.

BRIANNA WAS DELIGHTED to see Mrs. Winthrop and her son at the circulating library. She had just selected several gothic novels. The past few weeks were busy ones for her. Maeve insisted that she be fitted for new clothes among other things. But she still thought about the Winthrops and missed seeing them each day.

Viewing James again reminded her how masculine he was. He needed no padding in his coat to emphasize his shoulders. Snug breeches clung to his well-shaped, strongly muscled thighs.

There had been no invitation to visit the Winthrops since she came to Clarmont House. She decided to discuss the situation with Maeve when she arrived back at what was now her home. However, the ducal mansion never felt welcoming to her. It was too formal and austere.

Maeve was waiting for Brianna on her return, which proved convenient.

"I hope you enjoyed your trip to the library," Maeve said.

"I did," she assented.

"You must get ready for our fittings," Maeve said.

"More new clothes?" The wardrobe was already overflowing with day dresses and evening gowns. When would she even wear all of it? She hardly needed so many new things.

"Young ladies in London need to be well-dressed," Maeve said. "We will be having company for dinner this evening. That new gown with the gold overlay would be perfect. It works well with the gold in your hair. Let us put your hair up."

"I cannot manage it," Brianna said somewhat abashed.

Maeve smiled. "You need not do so. My maid is experienced with styling hair expertly. You will see."

That evening, as Jenine worked on her hair after Gwen did up the tiny buttons on the back of her gown, Brianna felt like a princess in a fairy tale.

"You look splendid," Gwen said with a broad smile.

Jenine nodded her agreement.

There was a knock at the door and Maeve entered. She too looked beautiful in a dark red gown which set off her fey eyes, shiny black hair, and olive complexion.

"Perfect," Maeve said. "You will be meeting some of our friends and family this evening. I believe it is time."

Brianna suddenly felt butterflies invade her stomach. "I won't have any conversation for them."

"Of course, you will," Maeve said reassuringly. "They are an unusual group of people. Not at all what you think they might be. You will see. Come stand and let me look at you."

Brianna did as Maeve requested. Maeve inspected her from the front and then made her turn around.

"How interesting. You and Adam have much the same strawberry birthmark on the back of your neck."

"Do we?" Brianna said.

"Now that you have your hair swept up, I have noticed it."

"Mama said it was quite ugly."

"It is not," Maeve assured her. "But if you prefer, we can get you one of the current stylish short hair styles that young women are wearing. It can be arranged to cover your birthmark. Of course, your dark golden hair is glorious just as it is."

"Allow me to think on it," Brianna replied. She was bewildered by all the rapid changes in her life. She had a growing sensation of losing her own identity.

"Let us go downstairs. Our guests will soon be arriving."

Brianna took her sister-in-law's arm and linked them together as they journeyed down. The duke was waiting for them somewhat impatiently. He was pacing the vestibule, but when he saw them, his face lit up with a smile. He extended an arm to each of them.

"Worth the wait," he observed. "Beauty always is."

Maeve gave her husband a pleased smile.

"I am sorry our guests tonight do not include more young people," Maeve observed.

"Plenty of time for that," the duke said.

"I suppose you are right," Maeve agreed.

"I usually am, my dear."

Maeve smacked her husband's arm. "You are also modest."

"Hardly, but a man in my position need not be perfect, only think he is."

They were soon joined by the Duke of Rundwall, a much older man, his son, Charles, the Marquess of Willingham, and daughter-in-law Lady Caroline. Brianna was pleased that Caroline and Charles were a warm and friendly couple who were also young, and she discovered they had been married less than a year.

"Like Her Grace, I will have my first child soon as well," Lady Caroline confided.

"I am so glad you were found. Maeve was distraught you must know."

Lady Caroline was well favored and of a sweet temperament. It would be impossible not to like her. Charles was a rough character, not a typical gentleman of the ton.

"So, Charles, have you been working out at Gentleman Jackson's Club of late," her brother inquired.

"Was honored to spar with him."

"Who is this Gentleman Jackson?" Brianna asked.

Charles looked at her in surprise. "Why, girl, he's only the bare-knuckle boxing champion of England."

"For all that," the duke said, "he has excellent manners and dresses like a gentleman. He's one of Prinny's favorites."

"You are pretty handy with your fives yourself," Charles said to the duke. "But I haven't seen you boxing lately. Gone soft, have you?"

"I have been working out at Angelo's of late, improving my fencing skills. But as Gentleman Jackson's is located right next door on Bond Street I will stop by."

"I will look forward to going a few rounds with you," Charles said.

Charles did look like a bruiser, Brianna observed. "Would someone explain who Prinny is?"

Charles looked surprised. "The Prince Regent. Thought everyone knew that. Where have you been living?"

Brianna flushed with embarrassment. "Switzerland," she replied in a small voice.

"Thought I heard something foreign in your accent," Charles said, rubbing his chin thoughtfully.

Caroline linked arms with her. "Don't worry about being taken for a green girl. I came here from the country myself not so long ago and knew little of tonnish ways. It does not signify."

Brianna was grateful for Caroline's kindness. However, she did not particularly care for Charles. Rundwall, the old duke, who was her brother's second cousin, was not someone she would have particularly liked to know either. His silvery hair framed a face as narrow as it was lined. His rheumy eyes were watery and myopic. He was dressed in the fashion of a young buck, which seemed inappropriate to his years, most particularly since he had the air of a jaded rake.

Soon they were joined by another friend of the duke. She was introduced to Lord Howard Randall. "May I present the younger son of the Earl of Caulbridge. Randall, this is my sister, Brianna."

Lord Randall took her hand. "Delighted," he said with a slight lisp. "Did not know you even had a sister, old chap," he said turning to her brother.

"Now that we are all present, I believe our dinner awaits," the duke said.

Randall removed a small silver snuff box from his jacket pocket, expertly took a pinch, and sniffed deeply. "Of course," he said. "Shall we?" He took Brianna's arm and led her into the dining room, following Maeve and the duke who led the way.

"I say, you are a great deal prettier than your brother," Randall commented.

She smiled at the foppish gentleman, accepting the good-natured compliment.

The evening passed pleasantly enough. After dinner, Maeve called upon her to play the piano and she was joined in singing some folk tunes by Lady Caroline who had a lovely voice. Yet Brianna could not help wishing that the Winthrops were here as well. However, she reminded herself that this was not truly her home. Her brother would not have been pleased if she took the liberty of inviting guests on her own. She would discuss the matter with Maeve, who was wise as well as understanding.

After the guests had departed, Brianna was ready to go upstairs.

"Wait for a bit," Maeve said. "There is something we need to discuss."

The duke frowned. "Is it necessary to do so this evening? The hour grows late. Are you not tired as well, my dear, considering your condition?"

"Yes, but this is important, and I did not wish to discuss it in front of our guests. May we go into your study? I wish for some privacy."

Brianna wondered what Maeve wished to discuss. "Perhaps I should leave the two of you alone."

Maeve took her arm. "This matter concerns you, and so it requires your presence."

After the duke shut the door to his study, he turned to Maeve. "You have roused my curiosity."

"Brianna, turn around and display your neck."

She did as she was asked.

"Do you see it, Adam?"

He gave his wife a puzzled look. "See what precisely?"

"Look at Brianna's neck."

He raised his quizzing glass. "She has a purplish birthmark."

"Yes, and it is similar to the one on the back of your neck." Maeve's silver eyes were bright.

"Many individuals have birthmarks," he said.

Maeve shook her head. "Not quite like this one. Did you not say yours was like that of your father? Do you not see? It clearly indicates that Brianna is your true sister, your father's child, as you are. She is not a half-sister or in any way illegitimate."

The duke stared at her until Brianna flushed with embarrassment.

"I have been perhaps unfair to you," he said at length. "As usual, Maeve sees and knows things others do not."

"Does it really matter so much?" Brianna said.

"It does indeed," the duke countered. "You will be a much sought-after heiress when we introduce you into society."

She had to wonder if her life would truly be better.

CHAPTER FOURTEEN

BRIANNA HARDLY KNEW WHAT TO make of this change in her fortunes. Truly, it must be very good. Yet why did she not feel better about it? The very next day, her brother invited Brianna to sit down with him and Maeve in his study.

"I have been giving your situation much thought," he said. "We cannot provide you with a proper come-out in the next few months. With Maeve so heavy with child, there's no question of us having a ball here at present."

"I do not expect or care for such," she assured him.

"That does not mean we cannot provide you with appropriate activities. I have asked Howard, Lord Randall, to act as an escort so that you may attend the theatre, the opera, and other enjoyable entertainments. He is a good, reliable fellow. Who knows? He might decide to offer for you. He is an eligible parti and a pink of the ton, a swell of the first stare."

Brianna did not comment. It was true that Lord Randall had a kind though homely face, but she did not feel the slightest attraction to him. The duke meant well. Somehow, she could not explain her lack of interest in Lord Randall to her brother. He was so stern, boot-faced. She said nothing, resolving to discuss the matter with Maeve as soon as possible.

The opportunity to speak privately with Maeve arose the next day. Brianna had just finished writing letters to be posted to her teachers in Switzerland. It was late morning and she felt certain Maeve was about. She knocked at the door of Maeve's room but got no answer.

Downstairs in the hall, she encountered the butler. "Where would Her Grace be?"

"I believe in the sunroom that looks out on the gardens, my lady."

She took off in that direction. The butler called something after her, but Brianna wasn't listening. Her thoughts focused on what she wanted to discuss with Maeve. When she opened the door to the sunroom, Brianna realized what the butler was trying to tell her.

The duke sat on a divan. Maeve was on his lap. His hands were on her breasts. They were kissing passionately, so lost in each other that neither was immediately aware of her entering the room. Brianna turned to leave so quickly that she lost her balance and banged into the door. The startled couple looked up.

"I will come back later," Brianna said, feeling the heat rise to her cheeks.

"No," Maeve said. "Please come and sit down."

Neither the duke nor the duchess seemed at all nonplussed by the situation. Maeve righted her bodice over her ample bosom and rose from her husband's lap.

"Actually, I am keeping my man of affairs waiting I believe." The duke turned to Maeve, gave her an affectionate kiss on the hand, and then strode toward the door. Then he looked back to his wife. "We will finish our conversation later. Good day, ladies." He offered the incline of his head and then closed the door with finality.

Brianna was abashed. "I do apologize for intruding on you and the duke."

Maeve waved her hand in the air as though swatting what she considered an unnecessary apology away as if it were merely an annoying housefly. "Adam is quite passionate. Do not be embarrassed. Our courtship was a tempestuous one. Our marriage has lived up to that expectation."

"I am a bit surprised. The duke struck me as being conservative in nature."

"Having a wife who is half-gypsy has heated his blood. I wish for you a man who finds you that desirable and irresistible as well."

Brianna lowered her eyes. "I doubt that would be possible."

"Life has many surprises in store for you," Maeve said with an enigmatic smile. "Do not despair."

"Do you read fortunes?" Brianna asked.

"Sometimes. I can read both tea leaves and tarot cards. They tell me things. Sometime in the future, I will do a reading for you, but only when you truly wish it and are ready."

Brianna did not comment. Things of that nature were beyond her ken. Did Maeve truly have such abilities? She could but wonder. Brianna decided it was time to change the subject.

"I was seeking you to ask if we might invite the Winthrops to tea. I would very much like to visit with them again. I feel it would only be proper if the invitation came from you, since this is your home."

Maeve invited Brianna to sit beside her on the divan. "It would be my pleasure, but this is now your home too. You have every right to invite your friends."

Brianna shook her head. "I have no friends. As you know, I did not grow up in England."

"We must remedy that as soon as possible. Ordinarily, I would be planning a proper come-out for you. But Adam is so protective of me and my condition that our social activities are limited."

"I do not wish for any of the so-called required activities. I want to keep my life simple."

"Your brother may have other plans for you. He has expressed to me the desire to provide you with a fine match now that he is certain you are his father's child. That will necessitate you being presented at Almack's and at court."

Brianna shook her head. "I do not see the necessity." Drawing attention to herself would only remind others in society of the scandal related to her mother. It would shame her as well. She did not wish for such notoriety and possible humiliation. She wished to live quietly and modestly.

Maeve squeezed her hand. "We do need to discuss this now. Adam is thinking of the coming season, not the present one. You need not worry. Perhaps by then, you will have found your own match."

"I am in no hurry for that either," Brianna said.

CHAPTER FIFTEEN

"Mother, I do not see why I must attend you at tea today when you are perfectly capable of taking our coach with the accompaniment of your maid."

James Winthrop knew he was being peevish and that made him even more irritable. However, he had little use for haughty aristocrats like the Duke of Clarmont. He did not wish to enter that man's townhouse again. His family wealth did not merely equal that of the duke whose means came from being landed gentry. His wealth exceeded that since his own came from investments in industry and shipping. He doubted the pompous aristocrat was aware of that fact as he looked down his long nose at those who were not born into titles.

If he were truly honest with himself, he would have to admit that he did wish to see Brianna again. But he was not a masochist, and the mere sight of what and who he could not have was troubling. He desired her. He missed her every bit as much as his mother did. He would choose to marry her if he could, but that was impossible as he knew so well.

The duchess and Brianna received them in the drawing room as before. The duchess was warm and friendly. His mother was immediately put at ease. When the ladies were seated, he stood by the fireplace, cold at this time of the year.

"Cook has provided us with the most delicious raspberry scones this afternoon," the duchess said. "Please enjoy them while they are still fresh and at their best."

James felt out of place as the women chatted about books they had been reading. He found himself pacing the room. He tried not to look at Brianna. Her eyes he noticed were cast downward and she spoke little either.

"Brianna must come and visit me," Mrs. Winthrop said. "I miss her exceedingly."

"So kind of you to say," Brianna responded.

"Not kindness at all, I do assure you, merely the truth. I will send you an invitation. I would include you, Your Grace, but I assume you are not getting out much these days."

The duchess smiled. "Unfortunately, my husband believes that women enceinte are so delicate they must remain at home. I am in excellent health, I do assure you, yet he worries. Therefore, I have become a veritable prisoner. We gypsies require our freedom, you know. Cages are not good for birds or people."

They finished their tea and the duchess and his mother chatted on amiably. He was growing restless. Her Grace viewed him with a steady, knowing gaze.

"Brianna, would you show Mr. Winthrop the garden? It is especially lovely at this time of year."

James was quick to respond. "That is unnecessary. Perhaps another time. We should be going."

His mother shook her head. "Dear, I would like to stay just a bit longer. Please take a walk in the garden. You seem restless. I am sorry I stole you away from your work; however, I will be ready to leave soon."

He gave a quick nod.

"Shall we?" Brianna asked.

He itched to take her arm, but he did not, merely following where she led. The duchess was right. The garden was indeed beautiful. It had a larger plot of land behind the mansion than he had expected. Summer gardens like this one were lovely with flowers and greenery in bloom.

"The roses are especially grand at this time of year," Brianna said. "That's what the head gardener told me. I like coming back here just to be alone and think."

The garden did not seem to be helping him in that respect. He could not think what he should say to her. His mind was in turmoil and confusion.

"Do you dislike me?" she asked in a small voice.

That brought him up short. "Not at all. Just the reverse."

"You were scowling at me."

"Was I? I must apologize then. I am awkward with women. I am not one of the experienced gentlemen you must be meeting."

She touched his arm, but then quickly withdrew it as if he were a fire that had burned her. "I am not really in society yet, nor do I wish to be. I have no need of fancy gentlemen."

They meandered through the garden, finally seating themselves by agreement on an ornately carved bench.

"I have thought of you a great deal," Brianna said, looking earnestly up at him with her large dark blue eyes.

He looked away and did not answer. What should he say?

"I–I am embarrassed to say that I felt strong emotions when we kissed. I had never been kissed before. Perhaps it is always so. I do not know, but somehow, I doubt it. Did you feel nothing?" She lightly touched his arm.

He turned and looked at her and swallowed hard. "Quite the opposite."

"I know I am being forward, but would you kiss me again? Just as an experiment, just to see if it feels the same. Please."

Something in him would not deny her or himself that pleasure. What did a kiss mean anyway? Surely, there was no harm in it.

James took Brianna in his arms and brought his lips to hers. Her breath was sweet from tea and pastries and something much more potent than either one. His heart beat faster with a staccato rhythm. The taste of her lips was like the most intoxicating wine.

Brianna was carried away by her feelings for this handsome young man. His tongue pressed against her lips and her mouth opened to him. Their tongues met. Their bodies melted together. Her breasts pressed against his chest. She burned from the heat of the passion she felt for him. Tentatively, his hands moved down her body, first touching then caressing her breasts. She felt her nipples tighten and began panting.

Suddenly he pulled away. "Please forgive me," he said.

She felt bereft.

"You are so beautiful. I get carried away. It is no excuse but true just the same." He combed his hand roughly through his dark brown hair.

"There is nothing to forgive." She lowered her gaze.

James shook his head in denial. "I do not wish to compromise you."

"You have not," she assured him. She felt such pleasure in his kiss and in his touch. Had he felt the same? She could not ask such a question.

James stood up and walked around the garden. She saw him take a large white rose from one of the bushes. He brought it to her.

"You are like this lovely white rose," he said, "pure and perfect."

She took his offering and felt a prick from a thorn on her forefinger. "I am far from perfect." She knew herself not to be pure either, but that was not something she could or would discuss with James. Painful memories were best suppressed.

He held out his arm to her. "Let us return to the ladies."

She nodded regretfully, stood up, smoothing her skirt, and placed her hand on his arm. Nothing further was said by either of them.

CHAPTER SIXTEEN

James was lost in thought on the carriage ride back to his family home. His mother hardly noticed. She was in high spirits, talking about what a lovely woman the duchess was and how much she enjoyed tea with Brianna as well.

"James, did you enjoy your tour of the garden with Brianna?"

"It was tolerable."

His mother threw him a knowing look. "Only tolerable?"

When he did not respond, his mother continued to speak. "I saw the way she looked at you and the way you looked at her. I believe there is true affection between the two of you. I believe she would accept if you proposed."

He was appalled. How could his mother suggest that? "Mother, there is nothing to discuss. The duke will see to it that Brianna is introduced to an eligible parti. In his eyes that would not be me."

"Brianna can make her own decisions."

James shook his head. "Let us not discuss this further. It is pointless. I know you want the girl back in our home but my marrying her is not the solution."

His mother looked downcast and that made him feel guilty, but she should realize that his decision was best for everyone. It was true that he had never been as attracted to any female the way he was to Brianna. However, that did not signify. No, the situation was impossible.

~♥~

BRIANNA SPENT THE next few days feeling restless and out of sorts. Summer days were hot, but the mornings and evenings were good times to be outdoors. Maeve also enjoyed the garden. They spent time planning the nursery for the baby that was expected to come in the early fall.

Maeve seemed to have a sixth sense. She understood Brianna's mood.

"We will invite Caroline today," she said a few days after the Winthrops' visit. "She is closer to your age than I am. She also knows more about what you can expect from society. It will be helpful to you."

Visiting with Caroline did prove helpful. She was a ray of sunshine, both in appearance and attitude. It was obvious her marriage was a happy one.

"We must arrange for Brianna to get out and about," Caroline said to Maeve, then turned to Brianna. "Maeve confided to me that you had a fit of the blue devils. No, do not be embarrassed. I too have felt melancholy from time to time. When I came down from the country, I too felt lost." Caroline gripped Brianna's hands in hers. "It is a pity that you did not arrive at the start of the Season. The Season always begins in March or April and ends by mid to late June when everybody who is anybody returns to their country estates and homes. But do not despair. The Little Season begins in September. Of course, society leaves by November. The town is deserted again by the ton. In January, Parliament begins, and many fashionables return to town since they find the country deadly dull in winter."

Maeve smiled at her friend. "I did not realize you had become such an authority on the subject."

Caroline flipped her glossy buttery curls. "Indeed, I have. But only since marrying Charles. Rundwall has been educating both of us. After all, Charles is the duke's only son and therefore his chosen successor."

"Adam is lunching at White's today with Rundwall and Lord Randall he has told me," Maeve said. "I believe a topic of conversation will be introducing you to society in small doses. Although we may be thin of company at present, they will be plotting, you may be certain."

Brianna rose from her gilt-edged chair wringing her hands. "I would prefer they did no such thing."

"Have no fear, Adam only wishes to introduce you to the right sort of gentlemen, no roues, rakes, fortune hunters, or scoundrels will do."

"Brianna you must be accorded an invitation to Almack's Assembly Rooms in King Street, not distinguished but considered the place. Exclusivity is the tradition there. Balls are held each Wednesday during the season. Low-level gambling is allowed. The patronesses issue vouchers to the chosen. Rank and wealth are important but not a guarantee of acceptance by the patronesses. They are very snobbish," Caroline confided.

"Which is why it might not happen," Maeve commented. "Adam's family is rife with scandal, including his marriage to me."

"I will ask Charles to discuss the matter with his father."

Maeve shook her head. "Your father-in-law has quite a reputation himself. None of us are considered good ton I am afraid."

"It does not matter to me," Brianna said. All she could think about was the passionate kiss she had shared with James in the garden. Did he think of her as well, she wondered. How lovely it would be if he wished to court her.

CHAPTER SEVENTEEN

THE FOLLOWING DAY, LORD HOWARD Randall arrived for a visit. It was clear that her brother had expected him to call. Ellis, their elderly butler, announced him, and Lord Randall was promptly led into the drawing room. Maeve rang for tea.

"How lovely to have you visit today," she said, with a bright smile.

Her brother joined them. "Yes, I agree. You are amiable company. Do sit down."

"Such a beautiful day, I took a walk, and my feet led me here. I passed a flower girl, and she was selling these. I thought you ladies might enjoy them." He handed Maeve and herself each a small bouquet of summer flowers.

"A thoughtful gesture," Maeve said warmly.

Brianna was relieved when the maid brought the tea service into the room. She was not in a mood to make conversation.

"Are you planning to visit your estate in the country?" Maeve inquired of Lord Randall.

"I believe I will stay here in the city for a time. There are activities to keep me occupied." He turned a quick smile toward Brianna.

She turned away.

"The weather is a bit cooler. Perhaps, Lady Brianna, you would allow me to take you for a drive in Hyde Park tomorrow morning. It is not the fashionable time of day, but the temperature will be pleasant at the early hour. You do not rise late?"

Brianna was about to claim that she did when Maeve spoke up. "Brianna always rises early. Our girl has not yet become citified in her ways. She has not been driven through the park yet either."

"Splendid," Lord Howard said with enthusiasm. "I will be here at nine tomorrow morning. I have a new phaeton. It offers excellent views."

THE FOLLOWING MORNING, Brianna found no one down yet breakfasting. She helped herself to tea and toast at the sideboard but found she could only manage a few bites of toast even when spread liberally with marmalade. She never lied to herself and would not do so now.

Brianna wished the person coming to take her out was James Winthrop. But he made it clear that he did not wish to have a relationship with her. Yet he had not disguised his passionate feelings toward her. She was confused by him. The attraction between them was real. Even a young woman of her limited experience could know as much. She resolved to see him again, to talk with him frankly. She would write to Anna Winthrop who would know more about what James was feeling and thinking. In the meantime, she allowed Gwen to help her dress for the morning ride with Lord Howard.

The gentleman arrived promptly at nine a.m. as promised. He was well-dressed in the first stare of fashion. The younger son of the Earl of Caulbridge removed a small silver snuff box from his jacket pocket, expertly took a pinch, and sniffed deeply.

"I will call my maid," she said.

Lord Howard shook his head. "Sorry, but there's no room for her as you may see." He extended his arm to her, and she took it, curious to see the vehicle he was clearly so proud of owning.

"The most spectacular phaeton is this four-wheeled high-flyer," he remarked.

The body consisted of a light seat for two, resting on top of two sets of springs and reached by ladder. She blinked. This was not what she had expected.

"Do not worry," Lord Howard assured her, noting Brianna's expression. "I will help you up there. I do hope you are not afraid of heights though."

She allowed him to assist her up to the seat, but looking down, she felt a trifle dizzy.

"Best set of bays around," Lord Howard bragged. "Cost a fortune at Tattersall's but worth it. I have an eye for good horse flesh. The stable on my estate is one of the finest in England." She thought his face was somewhat equine, in harmony with a man who loved horses, she supposed. Then she felt slightly guilty for mentally comparing his face to that of a horse.

"Do you ride, Lady Brianna?"

"No, I am afraid I never learned." Her mother mentioned riding in her youth, but the opportunity had never been available to Brianna.

"A pity," he said, "however, I am willing to teach you."

"Kind of you," she said politely.

"I am going to drive to the Northwest enclosure of the park first since there are cows and deer brought in for the summer months."

The sight in front of them reminded her of Switzerland and she felt nostalgic. He drove her to Kensington Gardens, which was beautiful, and then stopped by the Serpentine. The lake was lovely. In agreement, they left the carriage and walked there side by side.

'Oh, swans," she exclaimed in surprise.

"Yes, I thought you'd enjoy seeing them. When the season is on, I must take you along Rotten Row."

"What is that?"

"It is where the people of fashion ride to see and be seen. The ladies flirt with gentlemen and gossip about each other. It is amusing—and crowded."

Brianna shook her head. "I like it better here."

"Lady Brianna, may I presume to invite you to see some of the more interesting sights of London?"

"I will think on it," she replied.

He took her hand and kissed it. "You are charming," he said. "I intend that we will see much more of each other."

She was not certain how to react to his statement. Was his lordship intent on courting her? Perhaps it was just a request of the duke to which Lord Howard was responding. They were, after all, good friends. She hoped the matter was as simple as that.

CHAPTER EIGHTEEN

THE INVITATION TO HAVE TEA with Anna Winthrop could not have arrived at a better time. Brianna was feeling lost once again. Mrs. Winthrop welcomed her with open arms.

"So delighted you could come, dear. I have missed you."

"I have been missing you as well," Brianna said truthfully.

Mrs. Winthrop led Brianna into her cozy private parlor. "How are the duke and duchess doing?"

"They are well."

"The child is due soon?"

"Several more months I believe."

Anna nodded. "I remember what it was like when I had James."

Brianna wondered why James had been an only child. Had Mrs. Winthrop been unable to have more children? She would not ask such a question, realizing it was up to Anna to confide in her, but only if she desired to do so.

"I know both the duke and duchess are eager for the child to arrive."

Mrs. Winthrop smiled. "Are you enjoying living with them?"

"Maeve is all that is gracious, but I would still prefer to have remained with you and James."

Apparently, that was what Anna wished to hear since she nodded and smiled.

"We miss you a great deal."

"I doubt that James even notices I am gone," Brianna said wistfully.

"Oh, he notices, and he does mind, believe me." Anna drew closer. "In truth, I wished him to court you." Her face was flushed with excitement.

Their eyes met. "What did he say?" Her heart began to beat rapidly.

Anna shrugged. "He said that you and he would not rub well together. You are of a different class. He was certain your brother would not approve such a match."

To Brianna's ears, these sounded like mere excuses. Still, she felt a sense of dejection. James might feel some attraction to her but did not want her as a wife. "I see," she said and thought she really did understand.

"That does not mean we cannot enjoy each other's company."

"Of course not," Brianna agreed.

"Let us have our tea," Anna said brightly.

"I will play some music for you afterwards," Brianna said.

She did her best to be cheerful for the rest of the afternoon, but her heart was heavy. James did not want her. The man who had saved her life was distancing himself from her. She had no choice but to accept that fact. But it was so painful.

When she returned to Clarmont House, Brianna was summoned to the sunroom. Maeve was seated on the settee, her eyes closed. Brianna turned to leave so as not to disturb her.

"Do not leave," Maeve called out to her.

"I did not wish to disturb your rest."

"Oh, you would not. How was your visit with Mrs. Winthrop?"

Brianna seated herself next to her sister-in-law. "It was all right."

Maeve opened her eyes and studied Brianna. "What is wrong?"

"Why do you ask?"

"It is obvious that something is troubling you. If you wish to tell me, I will gladly listen."

Brianna let out a deep sigh. "It is about James, and it is childish of me."

"I doubt that," Maeve responded. She took Brianna's hand in hers. "What about Mr. Winthrop?"

"I felt a connection to him beyond friendship. I doubt he feels the same way about me. Anna, Mrs. Winthrop, would like it if he offered for me."

"She has discussed the matter with her son?"

Brianna nodded. "Apparently, she has done so."

"And he has not agreed to pursue a proposal?" Maeve's expression was thoughtful.

"In all fairness, we hardly know each other."

"Ah, I see," Maeve said, still holding Brianna's hand. "I noticed the way he looked at you. I do not need my tarot cards, or my tea leaves to read his feelings. He very much cares for you."

"Then why will he not court me?" Brianna shook her head. "No, you must be wrong. The feelings are one-sided."

"I do not agree," Maeve said. "There is something holding him back."

"Anna said that James blamed it on our differences in class. He felt the duke would never approve of such a match."

"My dear, that is probably true. Adam can be tyrannical and a bit of a snob. However, he did marry me, and I have a strong influence on him. James is an intelligent man. He could run off to Gretna Green with you if you both so desired."

"Elope? That seems so havey-cavey."

"It is often done under certain circumstances, but I do not recommend it. There is something else going on here. I am not certain what it might be. But I promise to make every effort to find out. I want to see you happy."

"Thank you, Maeve." Brianna felt tears well up in her eyes.

"In the meantime, you do have an active suitor."

Brianna threw Maeve a questioning look.

"I refer to Lord Randall." Maeve smiled.

Brianna shook her head. "He has just shown some interest in me because my brother asked it of him."

"They are good friends. That is true, but I doubt Howard would show you such partiality regardless of what Adam suggested if he were not truly attracted to you. Trust me, it is more than that. Why not give him a chance? Get to know him better. I know he is not as handsome or as young as James Winthrop. However, he is not unkind."

"I promise to keep an open mind," Brianna said.

"You will be the better for it." Maeve patted her hand.

CHAPTER NINETEEN

THEY DID HAVE VISITORS THE following afternoon, just as Maeve predicted. Lord Randall again came with bouquets of flowers for both her and Maeve. Caroline visited as well.

"I say, you ladies are all the crack," Lord Randall said, looking from one to the other as he raised his quizzing glass to his eye.

"Such fustian," Maeve exclaimed.

"A Banbury tale to be sure," Caroline agreed.

"Nevertheless, you ladies do love a bit of flattery, do you not?" he teased.

Caroline laughed, clearly pleased with his comments.

"Where is the marquess today?" he inquired.

"Charles is visiting with his father."

"Which one," Lord Randall asked.

"Oh, Mr. Brockton."

Brianna was puzzled. "Your husband has two fathers?"

Caroline glanced at Maeve who gave a slight nod of her head as if to say it was all right to explain matters to Brianna. Caroline shrugged.

"I suppose it is all right for you to know. Charles was the son of a French émigré who at one time was Rundwall's wife. She left him and eventually became Mr. Brockton's mistress. However, Charles was the duke's son, although he did not find that out until recently."

"Who is this Mr. Brockton?" Brianna inquired.

"William Brockton is the fellow who runs the queen of gambling clubs. The Prince Regent himself favors the place and is partial to Brockton," Lord Randall stated.

"Charles and I were both raised by him," Maeve said. "Perhaps I should explain." Maeve folded her hands and looked away as if her mind were wandering. "My mother was a gypsy princess. She ran off with my father who was the third son of a baron. They were not well-received by his family. My father was a weak man. He left his family, including my mother and me when I was little. We believe he decided to travel to America to make his fortune. But we never heard from him. My mother was heartbroken. She was treated terribly by the baron's wife. She died when I was six years old. It was decided to send me to an orphan home. That was the last I ever saw of my father's relatives. I cried every night. The orphanage was a dreadful place. Not enough to eat, rats running about." Maeve shuddered.

Brianna placed her arms around her sister-in-law in sympathy.

"Eventually, I ran away, much the way you did."

Brianna nodded and waited for Maeve to continue her story, realizing there was more to it. Maeve smoothed the skirt of her rose-colored gown which set off the dark wine of her complexion before speaking again.

"On a foggy night when I thought I would soon perish from starvation on the streets of London, I stood on a corner considering whether I might steal an orange from a street vendor. A man started to cross the street, and I had a sense of him being in danger. With my last ounce of strength, I pulled him back. A curricle came bursting wildly down the street. A drunken young buck barreled along barely missing the man. He was profuse in his thanks. He was grateful that I saved his life. That man was Mr. Brockton. He was only a fish monger in those days. However, he took me home with him and treated me well.

"He enjoyed gambling, but he usually lost at cards. Suddenly his luck changed. He began to win. He attributed that to me. He said I had changed his luck and brought him success. A few years later, he purchased his gaming establishment. This venture was also successful. Then he fell in love with Charles' mother. We lived together happily for many years. Sadly, Charles' mother did not live as long as we would have hoped for. But Mr. Brockton has continued to thrive. It was he who had me tutored and arranged for me to be presented into society."

Brianna listened to Maeve's extraordinary story with great interest. She had felt a close connection to Maeve from their first meeting. Now she understood why that was so. Maeve did not have an easy life. How her sister-in-law met and married the duke was puzzling. But Brianna chose not to pry into what was a private matter. Maeve was not a secretive person. Sometime in the future, Brianna supposed, all would be revealed.

"We are always delighted by a visit from you, Howard. But is there a particular reason that brings you here today?" Maeve offered an encouraging look.

"Yes, as a matter of fact, there is." Lord Randall cleared his throat. "I wondered if Lady Brianna would like to see some of the sights of London. There is much of interest in the city."

"I am certain she would like to see them," Maeve responded.

"Oh, splendid!" Caroline said, bouncing enthusiastically in her chair.

All eyes turned to Brianna. What could she say? She must not be rude.

"Yes, I would like that."

Lord Randall loosened his snowy neckcloth as if it felt tight. Brianna had the distinct impression that her brother had put him up to offer the invitation.

"I know the city well. Perhaps a bit of fun is in order?"

"I will come with you and perhaps Charles will be able to join us as well. What would you say to Astley's?" Caroline asked with eager intensity.

"An excellent choice," Lord Randall said.

"What is Astley's?" Brianna questioned.

"It is a wonderful place to go," Caroline said. "It will amaze you as it did me."

ASTLEY'S WAS A grand success, at least for Lady Caroline. She was enthralled with the equestrian performances. Her husband came and joined them as well.

Lord Randall seemed to equally enjoy it. "As a child, I had seen Philip Astley when that great performer had done his own equestrian acts. The amphitheater burned to the ground and has been rebuilt several times since then. With Philip dead, Young Astley managed the property and sometimes rode himself in the manner of his father. I enjoy good horsemanship, but my attention is drawn to other things today. Even the female performers in their skimpy sequined costumes and flesh-colored tights prove unremarkable points of interest. All I can think about is the lovely young woman sitting beside me. You are an amazing distraction."

Brianna felt her cheeks flush. Fortunately, she was saved from making a reply by Caroline's intervention.

"I do wish you had let us sit up closer," Caroline said to Charles. "We could see so much better up there."

"Only men sit on the front benches," Lord Randall said.

"What he means, my girl, is that you never see a woman sitting up front unless she's a whore. Those lecherous bucks come around to ogle the females in the show and make lewd comments. They're the kind that sit on the front benches," Charles said.

Brianna thought him astonishingly crude and vulgar but decided to reserve judgment. After all, the young man had obviously not been educated as an English gentleman early on.

Caroline's face reddened. "I suppose you are right."

Charles let out a deep sigh. "You should recall we had the same discussion before when we came here with Maeve and the duke."

"That was ages ago, before we were married. Oh, dear, look! How does she manage to ride so well standing on the horse's back that way? I am sure I could never do it." Caroline pointed to one of the riders, apparently once again captivated by the combination of circus, melodrama, and spectacle. Or had she merely wished to change the subject?

The gentlemen sat on either side of each lady. Lord Randall slipped Brianna's hand into his. Color rose to her face. She politely removed her hand from his. Should she comment? Perhaps not. Action spoke louder than words.

He bent over and whispered in her ear, "I don't mind that you are a bit strait-laced, in fact, I rather like it. One does not wish to show an interest in a lady who spreads her favors too liberally."

CHAPTER TWENTY

In the days that followed, Lord Randall was a frequent visitor to the ducal mansion. Often, it was to visit the duke, but he always contacted her as well.

"Lady Brianna, your brother informs me that you are somewhat of a bluestocking. You enjoy reading above all else or so he says."

"I would not call myself a bluestocking precisely. However, I do enjoy reading."

"Can not say I feel the same, but I do respect someone with other interests than my own. Would you like to see the Tower of London? Perhaps history fascinates you as well. Some go there to see the beasts. The lions are ferocious creatures. Oh, and the Crown Jewels! They are magnificent. You might even see Anne Boleyn's ghost. A friend insists he sighted her atop a tower on his visit." Brianna could not help but enjoy his exuberance. "Of course, the Tower is not just one building but many. It will take a rare bit of time to see all of that."

Maeve was listening as well. "Brianna might enjoy a visit to the National Gallery. There are many paintings by famous artists hanging there."

"Bit of a snooze, don't you think?" Lord Randall said, a note of skepticism in his voice.

"Not really," Maeve replied.

"I suppose we might see The Elgin Marbles."

Brianna was puzzled. "What are they?"

"A collection of ancient Greek sculptures from the Parthenon and other structures from Athens removed and shipped to Britain by agents of the Earl of Elgin."

"I understand it is quite impressive," Maeve said.

"But controversial just the same," Lord Randall said.

"How so?" Brianna asked.

"Lord Byron likened Elgin's actions to be nothing short of vandalism and looting."

"Harsh words," the duke observed as he came into the drawing room. "Elgin stated he removed the sculptures with permission of the Ottoman officials who exercise authority in Athens."

"Nevertheless, the veracity of his claim is dubious," Maeve commented.

"You have read about it?" the duke asked his wife.

"I have. It interests me."

"I shall take Lady Brianna to see the Marbles forthwith," Lord Randall resolved.

"Try not to be too shocked," Maeve whispered to Brianna.

She was puzzled by her sister-in-law's comment.

The following day when Lord Randall took her to the British Museum, Brianna understood Maeve's comment.

"My goodness, those sculptures are undressed," she said in surprise and embarrassment.

"Yes, they are divinely naked, human in all details."

Many other people had come to see the display and exclaim over it.

"You are shocked?" Lord Howard asked.

"I am not a prude, but yes, I find the statues surprising."

"I daresay you have not been exposed much to Greek and Roman art then."

Brianna realized that her knowledge was limited.

In the coming weeks, Brianna found she was out of her depth in many respects. London was a world unto itself. For the wealthy it was a fairyland of a sort, she quickly learned. But for many residents, there was poverty and desperation.

She discussed the matter with Maeve one afternoon. "Before Mr. Brockton took you in, Maeve, you mentioned you were in an orphanage."

Maeve looked up from her embroidery. "Yes, I decided to do something about it when I had the means available to me.

I took the children from the orphanage and brought them to Mr. Brockton's home where they trained for service. As one was placed, another was brought in. However, now that I am married to Adam, I can do much more. I purchased the orphanage and made it into a proper place for the girls to live. We have good teachers working there now. Perhaps you will visit one day? You could offer music or art lessons if you wish."

Brianna nodded. "I should like nothing better. I could teach there at least part of the time. I did so at my school in Switzerland."

Maeve smiled with pleasure. "That would be wonderful."

The duke joined them, and Maeve told him about Brianna's offer. He groaned.

"My mother and I agree on very little. However, on this subject, happens we both are of a similar mind. It is hardly proper for a lady to be teaching at an orphanage, or any school for that matter."

"I disagree," Maeve said in a firm voice. "Being useful is always proper."

Brianna felt distinctly uncomfortable. "I did not mean to cause dissention between you. Perhaps we can discuss this at another time."

"Very well," the duke said frowning.

Brianna rose to leave the room, but her brother put out a hand to halt her departure. "I want to talk to you about something. Howard tells me you and he have been spending quite a bit of time together."

This was a subject she had hoped to avoid. But both her brother and Maeve were looking at her with fixed expressions.

"Yes, we have walked and ridden in Hyde Park on several occasions. He has taken me to more than one place of interest in the city."

"He informs me that he enjoys your company."

Brianna wet her lips which suddenly felt very dry. "I enjoy his company as well. But I have the distinct impression that you are the cause of your friend acting as my tour guide."

"I might have encouraged him to do so at first," her brother said with a shrug, "however, it was entirely his decision to continue to see you. He is quite a fine fellow. Frankly, I think he would make a woman an excellent husband."

Brianna did not like where the conversation was leading. "I must tell you, I do not think of Lord Randall in that way."

"Well, perhaps you should do so."

Brianna quickly left the drawing room, not wishing to pursue the subject further. She did not want to argue with her brother. At the same time, she refused to accept him bullying her. She had some thinking to do.

CHAPTER TWENTY-ONE

THE TOPIC OF HER LAST conversation with her brother arrived to take her out the following afternoon. It was a lovely day, and the drive was pleasant. They stopped by the water for a time and watched the swans.

"I do wish I had an easel with me. Then I could paint this scene," she exclaimed. "It is so beautiful."

Lord Randall took her hand in his. "You are more beautiful than the sunlight."

She laughed at that. "False flattery?"

"Not at all. Not a bag of moonshine. I am no poet, but I know beauty when I see it. Perhaps it is time I was leg shackled."

Brianna turned away from him. "Did my brother put you up to this?"

"What? No, he would not do such a thing. Entirely my thoughts. I did not mean to put you on the spot so to speak. Let us discuss where we will be going on our next outing. I am thinking of introducing you to Vauxhall."

"Vauxhall?" she repeated.

"A place of great pleasure. I can almost guarantee you will enjoy it."

When they returned to the ducal residence, Caroline was visiting with Maeve in the sunroom. She and Lord Randall joined them.

"I was just telling Maeve about the new gown I am having made. It will be splendid, but I have nowhere to wear it at present."

"That can easily be remedied," Lord Randall said. "I was just telling Lady Brianna that I want to introduce her to Vauxhall. Perhaps you and Charles would attend with us?"

"I am not certain a pleasure garden is something I wish to visit," Brianna said cautiously.

"Oh, do go!" Caroline exclaimed. "It is marvelous. I will convince Charles. We will have a grand evening."

The matter appeared settled before Brianna could even respond. After their guests left, Brianna turned to Maeve. "What can I expect of Vauxhall?"

Maeve was thoughtful. "Well, it is a romantic place. I went there with Adam and enjoyed it. They have many attractions. You would love the fireworks, I am certain."

Brianna nodded. Perhaps she would have a good time. However, she did not wish to encourage romantic notions in Lord Randall. It would not be fair to either of them.

That night, she woke up at midnight, remembering a dream, a very pleasant one. James Winthrop held her in his arms, and they were kissing passionately as they had done before. She was consumed by desire. Why could she not feel the same emotions for Lord Randall? James was not courting her, most likely he never would. It was frustrating. Feelings simply defied logic. They made no sense at all. It was several hours before she fell asleep again.

SEVERAL EVENINGS LATER, Caroline and Charles arrived in an elegant coach accompanied by Lord Randall. All three were in high spirits. The gentlemen were dressed to the nines. Caroline was regal in appearance. She wore a thin, white muslin shot with gold, bodice, and sleeves done up with seed pearls. A pearl necklace and earrings completed the ensemble. Her golden hair was dressed in an upsweep with soft curls dangling over each ear. By comparison, Brianna felt a frump. Her plain white muslin gown was simple and modestly styled. Unlike Caroline, she wore no jewelry, nor did she own any.

Brianna was unprepared for Vauxhall Gardens. It truly was magical. Each walk was tree and bush-lined.

"What an amazing place," she exclaimed.

"Shall I tell you more about it?" Lord Randall inquired.

"Yes, please do."

He smiled at her, obviously pleased by her enthusiasm.

"The Grand Walk extends nine hundred feet from the entrance, thirty feet wide and bordered with elm trees. The South Walk runs parallel to it. There are graveled promenades. Concerts are held in the evening between walkways at The Grove. Fireworks are set off at 9 p.m. A bell is rung to indicate the cascade is about to begin during the intermission for the concert. The great waterfall tumbles over rocks into a frothy pool below. It is a rare sight to enjoy." Lord Randall explained all of this with the pleasure born of his superior knowledge. She realized he was attempting to impress her.

They walked to their supper box and were seated. Brianna had no complaints. The food served was of a fine quality, particularly the thinly sliced ham and strawberries. Caroline might be a bit scatter-brained and Charles somewhat uncouth, but they were good company all the same. The couple took a walk during the orchestra's intermission.

Lord Randall turned to Brianna. "Shall we take a walk as well?"

They made their way along the gravel path. Lord Randall held her arm. Thousands of glass lamps were hung in the trees overhead and illuminated the walkway. Brianna thought it might be like a scene out of a fairytale or *The Arabian Nights*. She paused to study some of the statuary.

"Not quite as impressive as the London Museum's Elgin Marbles but passable," Lord Randall remarked.

They walked further along the main path. Then he guided her to a smaller, darker path that seemed to meander through shrubbery.

"It is rather dark here. I think we should go back, or we will be lost," she said uncertainly.

"Soon," he said. "I want to spend some time alone with you."

Brianna was suddenly uneasy. "Lord Randall…"

"Please call me Howard. We need not be formal. I have admired you since we met."

"I must insist we return."

Lord Randall pulled her into his arms. He kissed her gently at first. Then his kiss became more demanding and ardent. She tried to place her hand against his chest to push him away, but he was stronger than he appeared. His hands roamed her body. Finally, she managed to shove him away. They were both breathless.

"I apologize," he said. "I was overcome with passion for you."

"Let us just go back," she said. Brianna hurried ahead of him. She fixed her bodice as she moved ahead, noticing that it had pulled downward suggestively. The pleasure garden had lost its charm for her.

CHAPTER TWENTY-TWO

THE FOLLOWING AFTERNOON BRIANNA RECEIVED a note from Anna Winthrop inviting her to visit.

She was eager to accept. The previous evening had upset her. Spending time with Mrs. Winthrop was always enjoyable.

They spent several hours sketching and water coloring in the Winthrop's Garden. Brianna demonstrated how to capture the essence of summer flowers.

"I am pleased with what we have done today," Anna said. Sunlight danced on the auburn highlights in her dark brown hair.

"Hello," James called to them. He studied the work they had done. "Lovely," he said.

"You are both talented artists."

"Hardly true in my case," Anna said to her son.

"No, it is true," he affirmed.

"Brianna is an excellent teacher."

James smiled at her approvingly and she felt a sudden fluttering in her heart.

"Would you ladies feel like taking a walk in the park on this beautiful afternoon?"

"Oh, do go with Brianna. I wish to arrange tea for us. I think some refreshments are in order."

"Are you certain you won't walk with us, Mother?"

Anna shook her head. "No, no, please go ahead. When you return, we shall have some delicious pastries with our beverages."

James smiled and nodded. He turned to Brianna after his mother left them. "She is not subtle."

Brianna smiled back at him. "But surely always well-meaning."

James took her arm as they walked to the nearest entrance to Hyde Park. She was pleased to be in his company once again. She observed he was dressed neatly in biscuit-colored pantaloons and a dark blue coat, most appropriate for a businessman.

"You have become famous," he told her.

She turned to him in surprise. "I have? How can that be? I am an unknown person."

"Not anymore. *The Morning Post* is mentioning you in their gossip columns."

She stopped walking and stared at him for a moment. "How is that possible?"

"You are the sister of a duke and you have been seen in the company of a lord who is a bit of a dandy and man about town."

She studied his manly profile. "How do you know all of this?"

He gave a small laugh. "Can you not guess? My mother of course. She follows you."

"How embarrassing!"

He narrowed his dark brown eyes. "It should not be."

"I am quite ordinary."

He let out a loud laugh. "False modesty does not become you, miss."

"Do many people read gossip sheets?"

"More than you might think. They thrive on bawdy, light-hearted stories about high-society personalities. Some members of the ton are so eager for flattering paragraphs they even pay to be placed in a story—at least that is what I have been told."

"How surprising."

"Just human nature I suppose," he said with a shrug.

Neither of them spoke for a while, both concentrating on their walking and admiring the scenery around them. Brianna saw an interesting Greek column and several statues. She paused to wander off and observe them.

"They are unusual, are they not?" James said.

"Quite impressive," she agreed.

"You are more impressive than they are."

James moved close to her, resting his hands on her shoulders. She realized they were hidden from view. She turned about to tell him they should return to the gravel path. But then she saw the look on his face and simply melted. Her lips parted as he lowered his head and kissed her, gently at first, tenderly, then more deeply. And it felt wonderful. So different from the kiss Lord Randall had bestowed on her. But then, as before, he pulled away.

"I should not have done that," he said. "I apologize. Something happens to me when I am with you. I lose all perspective. Are you a witch? Are you a magical fey creature?"

She could not help but laugh at such folly. "I believe you have bewitched yourself, Mr. Winthrop, for it is none of my doing. Perhaps you are a warlock who has designs on my person."

They walked on in companionable silence, each smiling, thinking private thoughts.

"We should have a picnic here one day," Brianna said as they neared the lake. "I could sit beneath the trees and watch the swans for hours."

When James did not respond, she turned and faced him. He looked sad. What was he thinking? "Is something wrong?" she asked.

He shook his head but did not reply. "Mother will be wondering if we got lost. We should turn back now."

Why the sudden distance between them? How could he kiss her the way he had and then behave with such indifference? She did not understand him. He was an infuriating man.

ARRIVING BACK AT the ducal mansion, Brianna looked for Maeve. She found her sister-in-law embroidering a white linen baby gown.

"You have a dab hand with needle and thread," Brianna commented.

Maeve smiled at the compliment. Her quicksilver eyes lighting up. "I enjoy thinking about the coming child. In confidence, I tell you it will be a girl."

"How can you know such a thing?" Brianna asked in surprise.

"I know many things. Of course, Adam wishes for an heir as all men do. He shall have one eventually. But this child will be a girl and I shall name her for my mother."

Brianna observed that it would not be a long wait. Maeve was clearly increasing.

"How was your visit with Mrs. Winthrop?"

"It was fine, Maeve. James appeared later in the afternoon. He and I took a walk together." Brianna looked down. "He kissed me."

"Did you want him to do so?" Maeve studied her out of the corner of her eyes.

"Yes, I did."

Maeve gave a nod. "You have feelings for him."

"I do." She bit her lower lip. "I am not certain he feels the same way. He appears to have reservations. I sense he has secrets that he will not share with me."

"Unlike Howard who is an open book. He, of course, would offer for you if you gave him the slightest encouragement."

Brianna sighed and threw herself into a chair. "Perhaps I am not ready for that."

"Perhaps not," Maeve agreed. "You are young and should have the opportunity to enjoy life. There is no great rush to marry, even if some giddy girls think there is. You should do what suits you best."

"May I ask an impertinent question?"

Maeve looked amused. "Those are the best kind. Do go ahead and inquire."

"You and my brother seem so different. He is, well," she swallowed and paused, "he is high in the instep."

"You mean somewhat haughty?"

Brianna nodded. "I wondered how the two of you came to become involved."

"I will offer the truth. Adam desired me as a mistress. I had no interest in fulfilling such a role. He chased after me. I led him a merry chase until he realized that marrying me was his only recourse. Even then, I did not readily accept."

"Thank you for telling me."

"My pleasure. I am always available to talk with, you know."

"Yes, I do appreciate that," Brianna said.

She thought of telling Maeve more about her feelings regarding James Winthrop, but realized they were at best confused. James took one step forward and then another step back. Still, she did not imagine that he was as attracted to her as she was to him. But there was much that she did not understand about James—or for that matter his mother as well.

CHAPTER TWENTY-THREE

"We simply must take Brianna to the theatre," Caroline said the following day, visiting in the drawing room.

Maeve agreed. "I would like to attend as well."

"Are you certain you are up for it?" the duke asked skeptically.

"Adam, you have me caged in this house. I am a gypsy. I need my freedom. Besides, I am in perfect health. There is no reason I cannot go out of an evening and enjoy a theatre performance."

"Splendid," Caroline said. "We can sit in Rundwall's box. He has the most perfect seating."

"Ladies, I bow to your pressure. You will have your way. I will invite Randall so that we have an even number."

The matter was decided before Brianna could utter a comment. However, she had never seen a theatre performance and did look forward to it.

The Drury Lane Company used the Lyceum Theatre which was performing *Hamlet* on the evening chosen. Brianna had read the play but did not enjoy it. Seeing it performed live was an entirely different matter. It was an exciting experience just to be present in a theatre.

The theatre was grand with an arched ceiling and two Corinthian pillars at each end. The body of the theatre presented a partial circle from the stage. The color of the interior was gold on green, and the relief of the boxes was a rich crimson. There were three circles of boxes above the pit.

People talked throughout the performance, which struck her as astonishingly rude. Food was even being sold by vendors. She disliked the distractions. Overhead there were many chandeliers lit by candles. It seemed the theatre goers stared at each other more than at the performers on stage.

"How do you like the play so far?" Lord Randall asked her at intermission.

"So much better than merely reading it."

"I prefer the comedies myself," he said.

"I think that lady in the box over there is waving at us," Brianna said. She started to wave back but Lord Randall caught her hand.

"Do not acknowledge her." His tone was stern.

He had never spoken to her in such a manner before. She gave him a questioning look.

Caroline leaned over and whispered in her ear, "That woman is a Cyprian. She is sitting with the infamous courtesan Harriet Wilson. Her box is used to flaunt her wares in soliciting and meeting possible protectors."

"How do you know such things?" Brianna asked.

Caroline shrugged. "Charles shares all sorts of information with me."

Brianna again realized what a green girl she was, and how little she knew of the world she had been thrust into.

She was disappointed to see that the performers were not dressed in period costumes but instead wore current fashions. She mentioned it to Caroline who appeared disinterested.

Her brother tapped Lord Randall on the shoulder. "Are you up for some shooting at Manton's gallery tomorrow?"

"A fine idea if you will join me at Tattersall's. I fancy looking at some horse flesh."

As Brianna studied the people in other boxes, she caught sight of the Winthrops and waved to them. The duke noticed and frowned at her.

"You should not be encouraging those people," he said.

Brianna was offended. "Why not? They have been very good to me. James and Anna saved my life. I could not ask for better friends."

Maeve leaned over. "You are a bit of a snob, Adam. It is unjust."

"Only my wife is allowed to speak to me thus," he said. He gave Brianna a sharp look.

~♥~

James saw Brianna. He did not respond with any form of recognition. But his mother waved back to her and smiled.

"Does not Brianna look lovely, James? How good to see her out and about."

He did not respond. She did look beautiful. He would love to take her into his arms and kiss her again and again. But he was a realist. It was impossible. Even if her brother would approve as her guardian, a match would not be possible. Well, perhaps it was possible, he conceded, but it would be wrong on many levels. He had to accept that.

"You are a very good son," his mother said. "But I wish you would take a wife. You need more people in your life." She patted his hand.

James shook his head. "Mother, I disagree. I work with people every day. I am not lonely." He hoped that would end the discussion.

"That is not the same. Perhaps we should visit with Brianna while the intermission continues."

"Perhaps not. I doubt those people with her would appreciate it."

"Her Grace is quite friendly."

"She is the exception."

James was relieved when the performance continued. He was of the opinion he had something in common with Hamlet. They were both melancholy and missed their fathers. But he at least had a good and faithful mother, even if she could be meddlesome at times.

The theatre smelled heavily of oranges and an undertone of stale beer. Members of the ton, dressed in the height of fashion, jewels glittering, sat in boxes. Lower classes and younger gentlemen of the town crowded onto floor benches downstairs. Girls selling oranges moved between the rows with an occasional squeal at being pinched or slapped on the bottom by a young buck. James would not have chosen to come here if his mother had not asked it of him.

Despite himself, James could not help catching glimpses of Brianna. He felt a sense of longing and loss. If only he could offer for her. But he could not, would not. It was out of the question. There was no point explaining that to his mother or Brianna. She would marry soon enough, likely to the dandy of the beau monde who sat beside her this evening, or another of his kind. Her brother would insist on it. He felt a stab of pain close to his heart.

CHAPTER TWENTY-FOUR

Brianna came downstairs in the late afternoon after writing a long letter to her former teachers. She missed them both. She found Maeve and the duke intent on a game of whist with Caroline and Charles. They looked up as she entered the drawing room.

"Would you like to take over my hand?" Maeve asked.

Brianna shook her head. "I am not much one for cards," she said. "I will go to the music room and play the piano for a while if you will excuse me."

"Of course," Maeve said. "Caroline and I were discussing a picnic in the garden for tomorrow."

"That sounds lovely," Brianna said.

At that moment, the butler entered the room and announced the arrival of Lord Randall who was fast on his heels.

"By George, the Thames stinks! Do not know why we stay in London when we could be rusticating in the country at this time of year." He threw his riding gloves on a cherry wood end table.

"It is my fault," Maeve said. "I choose not to leave the city."

"Well, God knows it was a bad winter. The city was preferable." Lord Randall turned to Brianna as if to explain. "The snow was falling on Easter Sunday, April the fourteenth in London. Even spring was wet and cold this year."

"The summers are very pleasant in Zurich," Brianna said with a note of nostalgia. She did miss her uncomplicated life in Switzerland. She had felt safe and secure there.

Charles stood up and walked around Lord Randall, eyes narrowing. "Fancy clothes."

"Like them? I just had this made for me at Weston's." Howard turned to display his slim-fitting double-breasted coat, which had a silk velvet collar and gilt buttons matching his gold waistcoat. "Weston is Beau Brummell's tailor you know, as well as that of the Prince Regent."

"The word is Brummell's fled to France. He owed thousands in gambling debts. If I'd still been in the collecting business, it would not have happened. That popinjay should be in debtor's prison by rights." Charles balled his large hands into fists.

Brianna looked to Maeve for an explanation.

"Charles used to collect gambling debts for Mr. Brockton. That was before we discovered his relationship to the Duke of Rundwall which was quite a surprise to all of us."

"I miss the old days," Charles said.

Caroline took his hands. "We have so much to be thankful for. Maeve has been wonderful. That is why I intend that we remain in London for the birth of your baby." Caroline went and hugged Maeve.

Brianna sensed that there was much more to Charles and Caroline's story, but she never asked questions of people. Some matters were private. Brianna did not discuss the years she spent with her mother before she was left by her parent in Zurich either.

THE FOLLOWING AFTERNOON, as planned, a picnic was laid out in the garden. Servants brought large hampers replete with cold chicken, strawberries, cherries, crusty bread, and wine. They seated themselves on blankets.

"This looks like fine fare," Caroline said. "I am feeling hungry."

Brianna agreed. The food was delicious. Their small group consisting of Maeve, the duke, Lord Randall, Charles and Caroline soon demolished it all.

"We must have a party," Caroline said as she tried to swat a bee away.

"What sort of party?" Charles asked.

"No balls here," the duke quickly interjected. "Not until Brianna is out in society. She must first attend the balls at Almack's Assembly Rooms. I will arrange for her to receive a voucher from that select committee of the most influential and exclusive ladies of the ton."

"Ah, the Patronesses of Almack's," Lord Randall observed. "That cannot happen until the coming winter."

"Parliament will be in session then, Adam, and you will be busy," Maeve said.

"Hopefully, you will be busy with our son," the duke said, leaning over and kissing his wife fondly on the cheek.

"You mean our daughter," she answered with a laugh.

"Either one is acceptable," the duke acknowledged.

"Surely, you can arrange for a rout," Caroline said, with a belligerent toss of her blonde curls.

"I suppose," the duke said less than eagerly. "Do you feel up for it?" he asked his wife.

"I am feeling well. Who should we invite?" Maeve asked.

"The Duchess of Pemworth nursed the ground for you, did she not, Maeve?"

"Indeed, she did, but only because she owed Mr. Brockton a fortune in gambling debts. He offered to rip up her vowels if she sponsored me in society. She complied."

"I am happy that she did so, or I never would have met you." The duke took his wife's hand and kissed it. "My guess is that if you ask Brockton to do as much for Brianna, the Duchess of Pemworth will comply."

"Everyone still in town will wish to meet your sister," Caroline said.

"Yes, expect quite a crush, old boy," Lord Randall agreed jovially.

Brianna was pensive. The thought of meeting a great many strangers caused her to feel uneasy.

"I shall get my secretary to write the invitations. It must be done soon," the duke said.

Later in the afternoon, Brianna decided to discuss the matter further with Maeve. She found her sister-in-law resting in her bedroom.

"I should not disturb you," Brianna said.

Maeve sat up. "I am only resting, not asleep. I find it difficult to nap during the day. But some quiet time is always welcome. Was there something you wish to discuss with me? Come sit on the bed beside me."

Brianna sat beside Maeve on the large bed covered by brocade silk quilting and pillows.

"Might you ask that the Winthrops be invited to the party? If you request it, I am certain my brother will agree."

"I will have a word with Adam's secretary, Mr. Nash. We will not trouble Adam with the matter. I think that is best. Rest assured your friends will be invited."

Brianna thanked her. As she started to get up, Maeve stopped her.

"There is something I want you to do."

Brianna raised her sandy eyebrows with a questioning look.

"Sometimes I have certain intuitions. I have one regarding the party we will be having. I feel that you will be in some sort of danger. I believe I can offer some protection for you." Maeve reached around her neck and removed the necklace she always wore. "I am going to place this around your neck. Do not remove it. It belonged to my mother, and it has unique qualities.

"If you should be threatened, the crystal on this silver chain will heat. It will ward off the danger in its special way." Maeve placed the chain around Brianna's neck. "I will let you know when you can return it to me. Until then, remember, always wear it."

Brianna hardly knew what to say. She simply nodded her head and left Maeve to rest. Brianna fingered the large crystal stone as she walked down the hallway toward her own room. The clear crystal felt cool to the touch and comforting. Did gypsies have magical powers, she wondered? Surely not. She could not believe so. Yet there had been something in the way Maeve spoke, almost as if she could predict the future, that made Brianna wonder.

CHAPTER TWENTY-FIVE

As Lord Randall predicted, the party at the ducal mansion was a crush. Since Brianna hardly knew a soul there, it proved perplexing to her. Her brother introduced her to many different people. She could scarcely remember all their names and titles. It was intimidating. When the duke finally left her side to talk with the older woman who had been presented to her as the Duchess of Pemworth, Brianna looked for an unobtrusive location. But clearly, that was not working well because a well-dressed self-important gentleman approached her. He looked down his long nose at her.

"So you are the one they are talking about," he said.

"I have no idea who that would be," she responded dryly.

He gave her a condescending smile. "You should be complimented. Everyone who is anyone will be gossiped about. The word is that Clarmont intends to provide you with a substantial dowry. In which case, you will have many suitors. No one will care which side of the blanket you were born on, my lovely. I know I will not."

She stared at him. "Are you a fortune hunter, sir?"

"Quite so. I am the third son of Baron Whiting. Supposedly I was meant to be a clergyman, but I do not have the calling. Simon Andrews at your service. I will be calling on you." He gave her a slight bow and walked away.

Brianna shook her head and then fanned herself. She hardly knew what to make of such a fellow. Well, at least he could be credited with being honest and forthright, she supposed. Perhaps that passed for charm among members of the ton.

When she saw Anna and James Winthrop arrive, Brianna let out a sigh of relief. It was good to see them. She hurried over to welcome them.

"I am so glad you could come," she said.

Anna hugged her. "I insisted James bring me." She made Brianna turn around. "You look beautiful tonight. Yellow is a much better color for you than plain white. Does she not look lovely, James."

Their eyes met. Brianna looked away first, feeling her cheeks flush.

"Yes, she is the most beautiful person here, other than you, Mother."

Anna laughed and touched him with her fan.

"You both look very well," Brianna said. "I believe you know Lord Randall as well as Charles and Caroline? Let us say hello to them."

"Dashed hot," Lord Randall said pulling at his neckcloth after greetings were exchanged. "I told the duke he should have the ballroom opened, but he refused. Said he did not want to do it until the season began."

"He will certainly have a ball for Brianna after she is presented at court," Caroline remarked.

Brianna did not even wish to consider what that would be like. She preferred to change the subject. In the meantime, a white-gloved footman dressed in ducal livery arrived with a large tray and handed each of them a glass of ratafia.

"I prefer wine, but this will do for now," Lord Randall said.

Maeve joined them. She accepted a glass of ratafia as well. "So good of you all to come this evening, Mrs. Winthrop and Mr. Winthrop. Brianna, I hope you enjoy yourself and your friends as well." Maeve looked splendid in a high-waisted silver gown that matched her eyes. Her shiny black hair was piled high with tendrils framing her face at each side.

They chatted for a time and then Maeve moved along to chat with other guests.

"I say, is that Maeve's necklace you are wearing?" Lord Randall inquired.

"Yes, she insisted I wear it."

"Surprising," Charles commented. "I've never seen her without it."

Brianna felt embarrassed. She did not want to explain Maeve's insistence on her wearing the unusual piece of jewelry.

She looked over at James. He seemed to sense her discomfort.

"I have been reading in newspapers about Britain's load of debt, our disordered currency, our slumping markets and rising unemployment. Lord Randall, are these concerns of Parliament?" Brianna realized James was deliberately changing the subject for her benefit. How considerate he was! And how handsome. His high, starched cravat was an immaculate snowdrift of perfect style, a contrast to the severe elegance of his black evening clothes. He looked as aristocratic as any gentleman present.

Lord Randall, dressed more colorfully than James, shifted his weight from one foot to the other. "Old chap, my father's the one to ask about such matters. I will not be a member of the House of Lords until the old fellow kicks up his heels."

Charles shook his head. "I haven't talked about such matters with Rundwall. His health is not the best. But it seems to me the country should be doing better now that the war has ended."

James appeared thoughtful. "I believe there is cause for concern. The poor seem more plentiful than ever, and the government hardly concerns itself with their welfare. There may be demonstrations in the future, some of them violent."

"Politics is a bit of a bore for a social gathering, do you not think?" Lord Randall said.

"I do not think we ladies should discuss religion or politics. They both lead to arguments. Quite right, this is not the place or time for it," Caroline said.

"I have been hiring as many returning soldiers as I can," James said. "The misery of the masses is obvious. My fear is that it will breed insurrection. We've seen it in Ireland. And the Luddites have again taken to smashing machinery in the Midlands. Next, there will be rioting in London if we are not careful."

"You should be running for the Commons," Lord Randall said.

"I would if I could afford the time away from business affairs."

Anna placed her hand on her son's arm. "Perhaps his lordship is right. This is not an occasion to discuss serious matters. We must celebrate Brianna's coming out into society tonight."

Champagne had just been brought out and Mrs. Winthrop raised a glass to celebrate. The others followed suit.

"Again, thank you all for being here tonight. I appreciate the support," Brianna said.

"Is Brockton coming this evening?" Lord Randall inquired of Charles.

"He does not visit here. Maeve goes to his house," Charles said. He was such a tall, strongly built young man that Lord Randall appeared short in comparison standing next to him.

"Why will Mr. Brockton not visit Maeve here?" Brianna asked.

Charles looked annoyed. "He doesn't have the time for such mainly. But he never was keen on Clarmont. Felt the duke stole Maeve away from him."

"And do you feel the same?" Lord Randall inquired with raised brows.

"Ain't my place to say," Charles replied in his rough manner. "They seem to love each other. Clarmont's good to her. That's what matters."

"Charles, they have opened the buffet table. Let us get something to eat. I am famished. The lobster patties look especially delicious," Caroline interjected.

"We will join you," Anna Winthrop said, taking her son's hand.

Lord Randall turned to Brianna. "Allow me to bring you a plate," he said.

She nodded her assent. Left by herself for the moment, she observed her brother standing across the room hovering by the carved marble mantle. Brianna thought of telling her brother how successful the rout was. That would certainly please him. She saw he was in deep conversation with an older gentleman. His back was turned to her, and she did not wish to interrupt, deciding to wait. She caught a snatch of the duke's words.

"I know my duty. My sister is my responsibility. I will bring her out in the coming season."

"Yes, a lovely girl. She will do well on the marriage mart," the other man responded.

Brianna was appalled. She hurried away. Did her brother consider her nothing better than a piece of cattle to be sold off as quickly as possible? Those were the implications of his words. She saw the open French doors and left the overheated drawing room behind. She needed fresh air and distance and took a few steps off the terrace into the garden which was lit by torchlight.

Venturing further into the garden, she breathed deeply of the surrounding rose bushes. She tried not to think of her brother. Was she a burden for him? She hoped not.

There was a sudden rustling in the bushes behind her. As she tried to turn, she was grabbed by a pair of strong arms. Someone caught her from behind, one hand caught her at the waist and another around the throat so she could not cry out. She tried to fight her attacker, jabbing backward with her elbow. She sensed a man, comfortable with violence. Fear strengthened her power to resist but the chokehold tightened.

"Ogden sold you to me," an ugly voice insinuated into her ear. "I paid him, but he did not make good on delivering the goods. I have come to take what is mine. I been watching you, waiting for my chance."

She stomped on his foot, but her satin slipper had little effect. She fought to free herself from this monster who attacked her.

"You are coming with me. Stopping fighting it."

She elbowed him and he grabbed the silver chain to tighten around her neck. As he touched the crystal, he yelled in astonished pain. It burned his hand.

For a moment, she managed to dislodge his fingers from her throat and screamed hoarsely. But he hit her with a balled fist to the side of her head. One hand tightened at her waist and the other returned to her throat. Her struggle grew weaker as blackness peeped around the corners of her consciousness. Then darkness closed in.

CHAPTER TWENTY-SIX

James wondered why Brianna had disappeared out onto the terrace. It made little sense to him. This was her party after all. Her brother gave it in her honor. Was she unhappy? He should not care, and yet he did.

He decided to follow her since she had not returned. He had the peculiar feeling that something might be wrong. As he walked through the French doors, he heard a woman scream. It was not loud, but it sounded like a cry of fear or horror. He hurried toward where it seemed to emanate from.

A man was lifting Brianna in his arms clearly attempting to abduct her.

"Stop at once!" James yelled.

The man turned only for a moment and then increased his pace, but he was slowed by his burden. Brianna appeared to be unconscious. James had a dreadful sense of déjà vu. It was that first day that he had seen Brianna all over again, but this was much worse. James caught up with them.

"Let her go!"

"No way. I own her. Get away."

James grabbed the man's arm, forcing him to release Brianna. The man who was not much taller than himself pulled a knife from a sheath at his waist.

"I will kill you if you do not get away from here."

James was undeterred. He would not let the fellow win no matter what. Brianna was starting to come around. She screamed much louder. People hearing the commotion began coming outside. There were concerned voices.

"What is going on here?" one of the men called out.

The knife-wielding adversary suddenly took off, running through the garden and out the side door fence. James wondered if he should follow the man. But Brianna was crying. He lifted her into his arms and held her there.

"Thank you for saving me," she said in a hoarse whisper. "He was a madman."

The rout ended early as word spread about the attack in the garden.

"It will be in the gossip sheets tomorrow," Lord Randall predicted.

"The Clarmonts are used to scandal," the duke said. "That does not concern me overmuch. What worries me is who attacked Brianna."

"He said Ogden sold me to him and did not make good," Brianna said. She rubbed her throat. It felt raw and hurting.

"We know who that was then," Maeve said exchanging an ominous look with the duke. "Dirk Foxworth."

"I will set my man of affairs Pritchard after him," the duke said. "We will not let him get away with terrorizing my sister. The Runners will be informed. We will have security established." He turned to James who had set Brianna on her feet and reluctantly relinquished her to Maeve.

Maeve was looking at Brianna's throat. "I have the perfect cream to soothe that from my mother's herbal recipe." She turned to James. "Thank you for saving Brianna. We are in your debt."

James shook his head. "I wish I could do more," he said with a heavy heart.

His mother joined them on the terrace. She looked from one person to the other.

"Perhaps we should be leaving," she said perceptively.

James merely nodded as he took his mother's arm, but he could not resist one backward glance at Brianna, just to reassure himself that she was all right.

"You are correct, Mother, it is time we left."

CHAPTER TWENTY-SEVEN

Despite Maeve's salve, Brianna woke late the following morning in some pain. Her maid brought in breakfast on a tray and opened the silk curtains.

"Her Grace supervised your breakfast herself. Everything soft, she said. Coddled eggs and blueberry muffins with a pot of tea." Gwen smiled at her. "Quite a lady is Her Grace. She will make a fine mother."

Brianna sat up and Gwen fluffed her pillows. "Lots of excitement last night. They are talking about it down in the kitchen."

"They are?" Brianna wished she could hide beneath the covers. Her voice sounded rusty.

"Oh, yes, Doris knows all about the fellow that went and attacked you."

"Doris?"

"You wouldn't know her. She works in the kitchen. A scullery maid." Gwen sniffed the air.

After Gwen left, Brianna slowly worked on getting down some of the breakfast. It was not easy to swallow because of the pain in her neck and throat. Later, she was visited by Maeve.

"I have brought more ointment," Maeve told her. Her look was sympathetic.

"I cannot believe that horrible man actually came here." Brianna shuddered.

"They will find him and bring him before the magistrate."

"Who is Doris?" Brianna asked after taking a swallow of tea.

Maeve looked away. "When we were frantic to find you, Doris found us. She had information to sell. She had been working as a maid for Ogen and his mistress. You may know her as Apple, that is her nickname."

Brianna looked up. "Yes, of course, she is a young country girl with apple cheeks. She told me that was how she ended up being called Apple. And now she works in the kitchen here?"

"Yes, I gave her the job. The information was not helpful after all, but she tried. Doris was also destitute. When Ogden left so abruptly, he made no provision for her."

"Do you think she might know something that would lead to that horrible man's capture?"

"It is possible. Would you like for us to talk with her? I could send for Doris."

"Would it be acceptable for me to go down to the kitchen and speak with her?" Brianna asked.

Maeve nodded. "We will go together. There is no harm in trying."

While Gwen helped Brianna dress, Maeve told her how successful the evening had been.

"Any number of gentlemen have left cards and floral arrangements for you, my dear. You have acquired admirers. Is not that wonderful?"

Brianna frowned. "It is more likely that word has spread about my brother offering a generous dowry. He wishes to have me off his hands as soon as possible I collect."

"Do not think such a thing," Maeve said vehemently. "He will do what is right by you, but that is only as it should be."

She and Maeve took the stairs together all the way down to the kitchens. Brianna had not ventured down there before, knowing it was not considered proper. However, apparently Maeve did not care about propriety. She did as she wished.

Mrs. Widmore, the cook, glanced up and then gave a short curtsy. Maeve looked at the girl sitting at the large wooden kitchen table. The girl looked up from devouring a bowl of bread pudding.

"Good day to you, my lady."

"How are you, Doris?"

The girl gave her a look of startled surprise. "You remembers someone as lowly as me? Why, ain't that grand of you!"

"Do you want to tell me something about His Grace's sister?"

Doris looked down at her pudding regretfully, as if she wished she could simply continue eating and not have to speak at all. "Yes, I have a bit to say."

With that, Maeve dismissed Mrs. Widmore and the lad whose job it was to help with the lifting and carrying. When they were alone, Maeve turned back to Doris. "What is it you wish to tell me."

The girl regarded first Maeve and then Brianna, head tilted to one side in a gesture of frank appraisal. Maeve sat down opposite the girl, ready to listen patiently to all she cared to say. Maeve offered no comment but nodded her head encouragingly.

"I was with them two years, Mr. Ogden and Miss Lizette. Served them very well, too. Wasn't my fault he ran up such huge debts. Mr. Ogden has a nice income, you know, an allowance from his family, but he can't manage to live on it. He's always gaming in the hells. I learned a little poem that fits him well: *Till noon they sleep, from noon till night they dress. From night till morn they game it more or less.*"

"I daresay that is the way with many of the upper ten thousand."

"I venture you're not like them, my lady. I seen you was different, that you cares about people."

"If that means believing those of sensibility should attempt to correct the injustices of the world as best they can."

"There, I knew it! You're nothing like Ogden and his whore. They care not a fig about others. Why, when his cousin brought Miss Brianna to him, all he could think of was what good it might be doing him. Mr. Ogden might have let the girl stay a bit, but he was only one step ahead of his creditors. He was desperate for money. He invited someone to the lodging, not a very nice man." Doris took a huge spoonful of pudding. "He goes by the name of Dirk Foxworth. Don't think Dirk is his real name though; some say he got the moniker because he were so handy with a knife. Anyway, Mr. Ogden owed him a great deal of money, and the bloke threatened to cut his innards out if he didn't pay up. So Mr. Ogden offered him Miss Brianna in payment."

Brianna felt sick to her stomach.

"Oh, it were very straightforward. Mr. Ogden would sign over the guardianship paper and in return, Dirk would have her."

"For what purpose?"

Doris looked flustered and turned her eyes downward. "Well, the usual purpose I would imagine. Except. . ."

"Except what?" Maeve's teeth were clenched tightly.

"This person, he runs these houses."

"What sorts of houses?" Brianna was afraid she already knew the answer to that.

"Brothels. But he owns this very posh place too, and I heard him say something to Mr. Ogden about how she'd do very well there indeed."

Brianna was horrified, yet somehow this was just what she expected.

"And did the transaction go through?" Maeve asked.

"I don't know for certain. You see, this Dirk fellow, well, he liked Brianna very well indeed, but he balked at the price. Mr. Ogden told him he wanted ten thousand pounds in addition to having his debts canceled right and proper. The fellow tried to bargain about the price, but Mr. Ogden stood firm. Then old Dirk said he'd have to think about it and let him know in a day or two."

"And where was Brianna while all this was happening?"

"Oh, she was right there in the room."

Maeve was incredulous. "And she said and did nothing?"

"Well, as to that . . ." Doris cleared her throat awkwardly. "I believe Miss Lizette went and gave her a drugged cup of cocoa, so she'd sleep through it all. But Dirk, he looked her over right and proper."

Brianna shuddered. She did not wish to consider what that might mean.

"Did the money transfer?" Maeve asked.

Doris shrugged. "Don't know, Your Grace. They gave me a day off, you see. Not usual but I was grateful and asked no questions. When I come back, Miss Brianna was gone and so were Mr. Ogden and Lizette. I never saw any of them again. Then word got around how His Grace was looking for information and would pay for it. That's when I come to you."

Doris looked from Maeve to Brianna. "I guess I'm not as much help as you'd like. Sorry." The girl hung her head.

"Actually, you have been a help," Maeve said.

They walked upstairs side by side, neither speaking for the moment. When she thought about it, Brianna was of the opinion that Maeve already knew the information shared by Doris.

"Nothing you did not already know?" she asked Maeve when they reached the sunroom.

"I am afraid not. That dreadful man is in a great deal of trouble. I believe he does have some powerful friends who frequent his establishments, but your brother will not let him get away with what Foxworth did to you last night."

"He would have carried me off if James had not intervened. James Winthrop has now twice saved my life."

Maeve studied her thoughtfully. "You care a great deal for that young man, do you not?"

Brianna lowered her eyes. "I do. I wish he felt the same about me."

Maeve took Brianna's hands in her own. "My dear, I believe he does. I am very good at reading people. I see desire in his eyes, a hunger."

Brianna shook her head, pushing back a lock of golden hair that fell over her forehead. "I do not believe that is enough. He does not love me."

"How can you be certain of that? I believe that he does. But something holds him back."

Brianna looked up. "What do you think that is?"

Maeve frowned. "If I could read his tea leaves or he would let me do a tarot reading for him, I might be able to find out. But I can readily see he does not believe in such things. He is a fine man, but a hard-headed businessman too. He is of a practical nature and does not believe in what cannot be proven. He lacks faith."

"Maeve, I am dubious as well of such things."

Her sister-in-law shrugged. "As Shakespeare said in *Hamlet*: '*There are more things in heaven and earth, Horatio, than are dreamt of in your philosophy*'."

CHAPTER TWENTY-EIGHT

SEVERAL DAYS PASSED WITH NO word about Dirk Foxworth. Brianna did her best to concentrate on other matters. There was much to be grateful for. Friends visited which was pleasant. They were considerate enough to avoid discussing the attack she had suffered.

"All will be well," Maeve reassured her at breakfast.

"Shall I return your necklace?" Brianna inquired.

"I prefer you wear it for the time being. Consider it a form of protection."

Lord Randall visited and invited her for a drive in Hyde Park. "We will take the gig down Rotten Row," he said, "and gossip about all the others that are doing the same thing."

Brianna declined. She was feeling skittish.

When the Winthrops arrived the following afternoon, she was in better spirits. Anna looked her over.

"You seem much more the thing."

"I am feeling better," Brianna acknowledged. She turned to James. "How can I ever thank you enough for twice saving my life?"

He shrugged and looked embarrassed. "I daresay anyone would have done as much. I just happened to be near."

"No, that is not true."

There were a few awkward moments before Maeve announced that the Winthrops must stay for tea. Brianna realized how much she wanted to melt into James' arms. It was no longer a mere attraction. She recognized she loved this man with her whole heart. But the question was: how did he feel about her?

~♥~

THE NEXT EVENING, Maeve had a dinner party for their close friends. After the meal, the gentlemen left the ladies as was the custom. Brianna joined Maeve and Caroline in the sitting room while the duke, Lord Randall, and Charles went off to the duke's library.

"They are going to indulge in brandy and cheroots," Maeve explained to Brianna.

"I cannot stand the smell of cigars," Caroline said, flaring her nostrils for emphasis.

Maeve appeared nonplused. "In the past, I never cared, but I confess these days it does make my stomach queasy."

"The baby is already smarter than her father," Caroline observed.

Maeve laughed. "I would not share that with the men."

They chatted pleasantly for a time. Eventually, Maeve yawned. "Perhaps we better get the men to join us for coffee or I will fall asleep on the spot."

"I will let them know," Brianna said rising to her feet as she smoothed her skirt.

"The butler can do that," Maeve said.

"No, I am stiff from sitting too long," Brianna assured her sister-in-law.

She made her way to the duke's study. The door was partly open, and she could hear them talking from the hallway.

"He ought to be shot," she overheard Charles asserting in a loud, angry voice.

"I could always call him out," Clarmont said.

"I would be your second," Lord Randall stated.

"But not the best way to handle this," her brother said. "We do not want any more gossip than has already been bandied about. It would just upset Maeve and Brianna. No, there are other ways to handle the matter."

"Such as?" Lord Randall asked.

"I would rather not say."

"What does that mean?" Charles demanded.

"I say, old boy, don't you know what Clarmont did during the war?"

Brianna leaned closer to the door.

"I wasn't told," Charles said.

"He ran a spy network for the Home Office."

"Not something I talk about," her brother said. "Let us just say I will be discussing the matter with my man Pritchard and the Bow Street Runners. Dirk Foxworth will not get away with what he did to my sister."

"I would like to strangle him with my bare hands," Charles said. He sounded fierce.

Brianna cleared her throat to let the men know she was there. They all turned to her as she entered the study.

"Her Grace insists it is time for coffee. She wishes an early evening."

"Come," the duke said, "we have been summoned."

Later, when Brianna was alone in her room, she thought about what she had overheard and felt troubled.

CHAPTER TWENTY-NINE

JAMES WAS FINDING IT DIFFICULT to concentrate on his work. He was thinking about Brianna and concerned that she was in danger from the criminal who had tried to abduct her. He dealt with difficult individuals every day, but they were not knife-wielding gutter snipes. He doubted that aristocrats such as the Duke of Clarmont dealt with such people either. He paced his office considering what he might be able to do to help ensure Brianna's safety.

There was one man he knew who might be able to help. Reginald Simmons was not someone James usually associated with if he could help it, but the man did work for the company. Reginald was always bragging about his success with women. However, behind his back, other men who worked for the company had mentioned old Reggie frequented whore houses.

James called Reginald into his office near the close of day when fewer people were about. Although the appropriate dress for businessmen in the office was black suit, white shirt, and neckcloth, Reginald, as usual, wore a bright yellow shirt.

James did not offer a seat to Reginald. He stood with the man, wanting this to be the shortest interview possible. He asked his question outright.

"A friend of mine needs to get in touch with a fellow named Dirk Foxworth. I promised to help by making inquiries. As a man about town, I thought you might have some knowledge of Foxworth's whereabouts."

Reginald raised an eyebrow, then rubbed his waxed mustache. "I say, I did not think you went in for that sort of thing. You struck me as a Methodist."

James sighed. "I wish to help a friend. Foxworth made certain threats."

"Foxworth is well-known in certain circles. He owns and operates brothels. I have had occasion to visit his establishment upon occasion—though not often. It is not necessary for me."

"Might you have his address? Can you write it down for me?"

Reginald studied him, then did as James had asked without further comment.

"I do hope this helps your friend." Reginald virtually leered at him before leaving the office. "I understand Foxworth's headquarters are located here. It is the address of his best house."

James took the proffered address without further comment. He decided he might bathe when he got home that evening. He felt dirty. He would probably feel even more so after dealing with Foxworth. He wondered if he should offer Foxworth a cash payment or threaten to kill him.

From the outside, the brothel looked no different than any other building in the flower district, although it was set back from the street and there was an ornate iron gate at the front. The impression was neither shabby nor elegant. James had no idea what to expect. He realized that he had been rather sheltered growing up. Although he had seen some of the worst and poorest of London's neighborhoods and rookeries, he'd never been inside a house of ill repute in his entire life.

It was not far from the theatre district of Drury Lane where unescorted ladies were unremarkable, in part due to the tradition of light skirts, actresses and opera dancers often found in the vicinity. James wondered fleetingly if the location for the brothel had been chosen deliberately to capitalize on the number of young women who came to London looking for success in the theatre, only to be disillusioned.

When he walked up the stairs and knocked at the door, it was answered not by a butler but by a young woman dressed in a low-cut, revealing gown of a gauzy thin poplin material.

It was obvious at first glance that she wore no form of undergarment. Her nipples were almost completely exposed. James did his best not to stare. However, the girl's manners were not as good as his own.

"Did you want something 'ere?"

"Yes, I am looking for Mr. Foxworth. I was told I might find him within."

The girl eyed him coldly. "Who wants him?"

"Is he here or not?" He stepped forward, trying to glance around.

"Just stay where you is for the moment. I'll fetch someone to see you."

James walked into the hallway and cautiously moved forward. He found himself in a large, opulent room. There were statues placed about, white marble figures of men and women done in Greek and Roman style. But the figures were presented in many forms of erotic congress, vividly graphic. Heavy purple draperies were pulled to keep out the light of day. There was thick, plush purple carpeting and comfortable chairs and settees all around the room. One wall was mirrored, and James caught sight of himself in it. He thought how out of place he looked in such a room.

The girl returned leading an older woman toward him. This woman was plump and wore heavy makeup. Her short, feather-cut hair was a bright, brassy red and she wore a damped-down bodice, which proved revealing of her generously endowed bosom.

"You was asking for Mr. Foxworth?" the woman said as she eyed James suspiciously.

"I was told I could find him here."

"What's your business with him?"

"That is between him and me. Now, is he here?"

The woman nodded. She turned to the girl. "Go fetch the master and be quick about it." She gave the girl a shove. "We don't need no non-paying men lurking about."

They were soon joined by Foxworth. In daylight, James could see that Foxworth was short in stature and rapier thin but carried himself like a strutting rooster. His mode of dress was pretentious in the first stare of London fashion. Foxworth had cold, light blue eyes that narrowed sharply to examine his own and probe their depths.

"Louise, I'll take it from here. You have a great deal to do getting ready for tonight. We'll be busy in short order."

The woman Foxworth called Louise gave him a final nasty look before leaving them.

"What is it you want?" Foxworth said with directness.

"I want you to stay away from Lady Brianna."

Foxworth gave an ugly laugh. "I own that girl. Ogden took my money and cheated me. I intend to collect."

"I will pay you off."

Foxworth shook his head. "Not good enough."

"You will come to regret this."

"This is my place of business. Get out of here and do not come back." Foxworth removed a knife from his boot and attempted to swing it in an arc.

James was too quick for the smaller man, knocking him to the floor. He left in disgust, realizing that he had not accomplished what he set out to do. Foxworth had not been intimidated in the least.

CHAPTER THIRTY

As Brianna brought an arrangement of flowers into the drawing room, she heard an unfamiliar man's voice. She entered the room and found Maeve sitting with a man she did not recognize.

The man rose and gave a slight bow. Brianna curtsied politely in return.

"Brianna, I wish to introduce you to Mr. William Brockton, my benefactor," Maeve said.

Brianna observed he was homely, common-looking, and far from young. His sideburns were thick and gray.

"Maeve calls me her benefactor, but in reality, she is my benefactor. Maeve has brought me a life of good fortune and done so for others as well." He squeezed Maeve's hand affectionately.

"How nice to meet you, sir," Brianna said.

"The pleasure is mine."

"I am going to ring for tea," Maeve said. "I sent for Mr. Brockton today because I believe he may be able to help with your problem," she said to Brianna. "I have been explaining to him what happened to you."

Mr. Brockton shook his head. "A nasty piece of work is that Dirk Foxworth. I do not know him personally, but he has a deuced bad reputation. What I can do is to loan you Ralph."

"Ralph?" Brianna repeated.

"He is Mr. Brockton's stalwart footman and bodyguard. He offers wonderful protection."

"There is just one problem. Like myself, Ralph is not partial to your duke, Maeve."

"It will only to be temporary until we sort this matter out."

Mr. Brockton shrugged. "It will be as you wish, my dear. I will send Ralph to you tomorrow."

"Thank you," she said and kissed his cheek.

"Meantime, can you offer something to drink a bit stronger than tea?"

Maeve laughed. "Of course. Adam favors Madeira. You might like it as well."

During the rest of the visit, Maeve and Mr. Brockton talked about the girls she had sent him from the orphanage and how each was doing working in his home. The girls were being trained in useful occupations it seemed. Maeve helped place them when they seemed ready to move on.

After Mr. Brockton departed, Brianna and Maeve were joined by the duke.

"I will ring for fresh tea," Maeve said.

"Do not bother. What did Brockton want," the duke said scowling.

Maeve smiled. "I invited him. I barely see him of late."

The duke sat down beside Maeve on the settee. "He has as little regard for me as I have for him."

Maeve shook her head. "He is the best of men. I spoke to him about Brianna's problem. He will send Ralph."

The duke groaned. "God no! That man is rude and disrespectful."

"Ralph is a wonderful bodyguard. He will protect Brianna wherever she chooses to go."

"Hopefully, we won't have to put up with him for very long. I plan to dispose of Dirk Foxworth one way or another."

Maeve took her husband's hands in her own smaller ones. "I do not like the sound of that."

"Do not trouble yourself. The matter will be resolved soon."

Brianna rose to her feet. "Please do not act hastily on my account."

"I assure you. I never act in haste." There was a cold look in his indigo eyes that sent a chill snaking down Brianna's spine. She decided her brother was not a man to cross.

~♥~

As PROMISED, RALPH appeared the following morning. He was a large fellow, not as tall as the duke, but broader and clearly more muscular. Maeve introduced him to Brianna.

"It's a pleasure to be of service to you both." As Ralph spoke, he was moving, doffing his hat. For a man his size, he was remarkably agile. He had powerful ham hock hands, large and meaty, that were callused. There would be no way that he would fit into the livery of a footman, nor would it seem appropriate.

"We will be attending the Duchess of Pemworth's musical evening. She has engaged the opera singer Maria Martinelli to perform several arias. There will also be performances by the Marquess and his daughters," Maeve explained.

"Sounds boring to me," Ralph said, scratching his head.

"Now there we can finally agree on something," the duke said as he entered the drawing room. "Must we go?" he said to Maeve.

"I am afraid so. The duchess will prove an important connection if Brianna is to be introduced into society."

"I do not care about such things," Brianna said.

"So you have said. Never mind, we will attend." The duke let out a deep sigh.

"Ralph will remain beside our coachman," Maeve said.

"If I am to escort you ladies, perhaps Ralph's presence will not be necessary," the duke said.

"Beg in your pardon. I think it is, Your Worthyship," Ralph said.

"Kindly address me as Your Grace," the duke said. He turned to Maeve. "Is this person really necessary? Send him back to Brockton."

"Adam, I have a feeling, an intuition, that Brianna will need Ralph's presence."

"If there is a safety issue, perhaps we should all stay at home and send our apologies to the duchess."

Maeve shook her head. "No, we cannot allow that dreadful man to make us prisoners in our home. I refuse to allow us to be afraid."

The duke gritted his teeth. "It is not a matter of fear, only good sense."

"Brianna must have a life." In the end, Maeve won out.

~♥~

THE MUSICALE THAT evening proved an impressive event. The opera singer had a set of lungs that caused the crystals in the overhead chandelier to quiver and jingle. Madame Martinelli brought her own accompanist who played the piano with professional skill. During the intermission, he continued to play, joined by a young woman on the flute and a young man who played the violin.

The Duchess of Pemworth, her double chin bobbing, personally introduced Brianna to several gentlemen of consequence. Before the second part of the program could begin, the duke rushed up to Brianna.

"Maeve is feeling unwell," he said.

Brianna was immediately concerned. "Is it the baby?"

"I cannot be certain. She has discomfort. I must take her home."

"I will get our wraps," Brianna said.

"No, you need not miss the rest of the performance."

"There is no question in my mind that I wish to go as well."

Because Ralph was not expecting them to leave so soon, both he and the coachman were up the street with the coach parked. The duke left Maeve and Brianna to walk up the street and signal them.

At that moment, someone came from shrubbery beside the building and attempted to grab Brianna. She screamed. Maeve yelled for her husband who came running. Ralph was not far behind. Brianna elbowed her attacker and pulled away. The duke withdrew a pistol from his jacket and proceeded to aim it and shoot at the man as he ran through the alley.

"Damn it! I missed!" The duke turned to Ralph who had just arrived on the scene. "Where were you?"

"I were not expecting you so soon or I would have pulled up in front of the house. I am sorry, your worshipfulness."

"Just take us home," her brother said in an irritated tone of voice. "I will be meeting with the Runners tomorrow afternoon. We will rid ourselves of that miserable creature."

Their coachman and several footmen appeared to help them into their carriage.

"Are you all right?" the duke asked Maeve. His brow furrowed worriedly.

Maeve gave him a reassuring smile. "Just a bit of discomfort. Perhaps the music did not please our child."

"I thought it a bit much myself," the duke said. "Our child is already demonstrating discriminating taste."

~♥~

JAMES HAD DECIDED not to mention his visit to Dirk Foxworth to his mother. He felt foolish. But hopefully, his message had gotten through to the fellow and he would no longer harass Brianna.

Over dinner, that evening, James and his mother discussed the events of their respective day. His mother always took an interest in the business, something he appreciated. He liked keeping her informed.

"There was something I meant to mention to you," his mother said as they began their soup course. "I sent an invitation to Brianna to have tea with me tomorrow. It was declined."

James moved his soup bowl away. "What? Is there a problem?""

Anna leaned forward in her chair. "That horrible fellow tried to abduct her yet again. He is stalking her it would seem. She is not up to a visit tomorrow."

James felt sick. Clearly, he had not been at all successful in dealing with Foxworth. Anger rose in him. "Someone will have to deal with him," he said through clenched teeth.

"Now, dear, do not overset yourself. I believe Brianna's brother will handle the situation."

"Perhaps." James decided that Foxworth needed something stronger than a mere warning.

CHAPTER THIRTY-ONE

THE ORMOLU CLOCK ON THE mantel struck one in the afternoon. Brianna and Maeve both looked up as the duke entered the drawing room, his posture stiff, his stride purposeful.

"I will be leaving forthwith to consult with the Runners," he told them.

"I am going to come with you," Brianna said resolutely.

"What? You will do no such thing," the duke responded. He raised his chin.

Maeve lifted her hand in a halting gesture. "Adam, Brianna has every right to go with you. The Runners will also want to hear her story first-hand."

"I take responsibility for what happened. Had I not been in my cups and grief-stricken over the death of my father, I should probably have acted differently on the day my mother first brought my sister here."

Maeve walked across the room and placed her arms around her husband in a gesture of support. "Both Brianna and I have forgiven you. Your mother was as much to blame. Deep emotions are complicated."

The duke kissed his duchess on the forehead with feeling. "You always know what to say, my love. You are the best of your sex."

It was nearly two o'clock by the time the ducal carriage arrived on Bow Street. There was very little conversation between herself and the duke. Accompanied by Ralph, their stalwart bodyguard, Brianna and her brother entered the courthouse.

The duke asked for John Townsend. He had explained to her that he had confidence in Townsend. That Bow Street Runner had a reputation of being of the highest order and had even been trusted to escort the Prince Regent to Brighton.

"Townsend ain't here," came the abrupt response.

"Will he be returning today?" the duke asked.

Brianna tapped her right foot against the floor, caught herself, and stopped. It was difficult being patient, but she had learned courtesy and politeness at school.

"Not likely to return any time soon. He and some of the others are still out catching that gang of smugglers in Kent with the help of the troops."

The man facing them was short, with a puffed-up chest and jowls. He identified himself as Josh Williams. Brianna wondered fleetingly if he was trustworthy.

"Since Mr. Townsend is not available, I wish to see the chief magistrate, Sir Richard Birnie. You may inform him that the Duke of Clarmont is here with his sister on an urgent matter."

"Right, Guv," William responded, duly impressed.

It was not long before they were meeting with Sir Richard. Explaining what had happened to her was stressful and difficult, but her brother being beside her helped a great deal.

The chief magistrate listened sympathetically and without further comment and then issued a search warrant for the premises of the brothel as well as an arrest warrant for Dirk Foxworth. Two Runners were dispatched, and Brianna felt reassured.

"Thank you," Brianna said to the duke on the drive back.

He gave a regal nod and then patted her hand. "We will be able to put this unfortunate incident to rest soon enough."

THE FOLLOWING AFTERNOON Lord Randall took her riding in Hyde Park. It was a humid August day, but not unpleasant. Still, she would have preferred the weather in Zurich at this time of year. However, Brianna felt she was adapting well, all things considered.

Lord Randall did not ask about her experience meeting the Runners although she was certain her brother would have mentioned it to him.

"There will be many enjoyable events this season," Lord Randall observed. "You will have invitations to some elegant balls. Make certain you purchase many dancing slippers for you will be wearing them out."

She laughed at that. "You are that certain?"

He smiled, his homely face lighting up. "I will personally see to it, my dear."

Brianna fingered Maeve's necklace which she wore everywhere she went. "My life here is so different. I feel like a princess in a fairy tale."

"You are as lovely as a princess," he assured her.

Brianna said nothing.

"Would you like to walk by the river? I have brought some bread to feed the swans."

"Oh, yes, Lord Randall, that would be delightful."

"Please, I remind you that you must call me Howard. All my friends do so."

They walked by the Serpentine, feeding the swans and watching children at play, a scowling governess sitting under a tree close by. It was very nice indeed, an idyllic setting. Yet she found herself wishing it was James Winthrop who was walking beside her. She let out a sigh.

Lord Randall took her hand. "Your brother told me that matters are proceeding well, and the Runners have been set to outfox Foxworth. I hope it is not indelicate for me to mention it." He stopped walking and looked into her eyes, his own amber ones thoughtful and sympathetic.

"We can talk about it. I am not some weak creature."

"I would gladly thrash that man for you."

Brianna shook her head. "No, my brother is correct. It is a matter for the authorities."

"We will see."

For the first time, Brianna observed Lord Randall's expression turning hard and ominous. She found herself shivering although it was a very warm day. There was more to Howard than appearances would indicate.

CHAPTER THIRTY-TWO

THE FOLLOWING MORNING, BRIANNA WAS breakfasting with Maeve when her brother joined them. He chose toast and kippers from the sideboard along with scrambled eggs. He was served coffee when he was seated beside his wife.

"I hope you are enjoying a hearty meal, my dear," he said to Maeve, looking over at her plate.

"I am trying to do so. I was told the nausea would end months ago but it simply has not happened, at least not in the mornings."

"I wish I could do something to alleviate it for you," the duke said.

"I am sprinkling a bit of ginger on my buttered toast," Maeve said. "I do find that helps."

The duke turned to Brianna. "Any time you wish a remedy just ask my wife. She has an amazing knowledge of herbs and what improvements they can make."

"I learned from my mother," Maeve explained. "It is the way of the gypsies."

The butler entered the dining room.

"Your Grace," Ellis intoned with formality. "A gentleman from Bow Street to see you. I told him you were at breakfast, but he insists the matter he has come on is of importance to you."

"Please send him in," the duke said, rising to his feet. He rubbed his hands together. "It seems we will have some intelligence today."

Maeve turned to the duke after Ellis left the room. "It is too soon. I do not have a good feeling about it."

The duke gave his wife a condescending smile. "Maeve, if this is your insistence that you have some sort of paranormal insight, I am dubious."

She shrugged. "Believe what you wish."

Josh Williams followed the aged butler into the dining room. Williams eyed the laden sideboard admiringly. The duke took notice.

"Williams, please help yourself to a plate. I daresay there is plenty for everyone."

"Thank you, Your Grace. Don't mind if I do." With that, Williams eagerly filled a plate with a selection of everything that was offered. As soon as he sat down, the Runner began eating with gusto.

"Williams, what have you and your men discovered?" the duke inquired.

His mouth still full, the Runner swallowed hard. "Well, Your Grace, there's good news. We located Foxworth."

"And you have taken him into custody?" the duke interposed.

Williams shook his head. "Not exactly. We did find him by that fancy brothel he owns, but the fact of the matter…" Williams broke off.

The duke was impatient. "Continue, man."

Williams put down his fork. "Sorry, sir, but there are ladies present. Don't know if I should continue."

"You must," Maeve said.

"Very well then. We found Foxworth in the alley outside the building. He was dead."

"Dead?" the duke repeated in surprise.

Williams nodded.

"Of natural causes?"

Williams shook his head. "No, Your Grace, afraid not. We found a knife sticking in his back. He were face down on the ground. There were a large rock close by. It had hair and blood on it. Looked like he were attacked from behind, coshed on the noggin first, then finished off with a knife. We think the knife used likely belonged to the victim hisself."

Brianna turned to Maeve. "Your instinct about this was correct."

"I feel badly about the death of anyone," Maeve said.

"Not this fellow surely," the duke said. "Someone deserves a medal."

"We've got the killer," Williams said.

"So quickly?" the duke responded, raising his brows in surprise.

"Fellow swore up and down he didn't do it. That's what they all say if you follow me." Williams gave a smug smile showing yellow teeth.

"Who was it?" the duke asked.

"Fellow named James Winthrop."

Brianna was suddenly sick to her stomach. She stood up nearly knocking over her chair. "That cannot be! James would not harm anyone."

The duke took her hand. "My dear, how well do you really know him? I assume he spoke with Foxworth. Likely Winthrop threatened him if he came near you again. They must have quarreled and in the heat of the moment, Winthrop attacked the miscreant."

Brianna shook her head. "No, I do not believe that."

"Were there any witnesses?" Maeve asked.

Williams nodded. "Aye, there was. The madam of the house. Calls herself Madame Louise. She said Winthrop came around looking for Foxworth, and it were the second time he did so. She was not an eyewitness to the killing, mind you, but she said she saw the two men quarreling and then it got violent, and she told them to take the argument outside."

"I cannot accept this," Brianna said. She turned to Josh Williams. "Has James's mother, Anna Winthrop, been told?"

"Yes, we took care of that at the request of the suspect. We have him in custody. He'll have to go before the magistrate."

"Perhaps it was self-defense," the duke said.

Williams shook his head. "Afraid not. Couldn't be."

"They could have fought over the knife," the duke observed.

"Sorry, Your Grace, Foxworth's skull was fractured. He would have been unconscious when the knife stabbing occurred."

"This is too dreadful," Brianna said. "I must go to see Mrs. Winthrop right now. She is surely beside herself."

"Do you think that is wise?" the duke asked.

"It is what I must do."

"Of course, you are right," Maeve said decisively. "You must go, but Ralph will go with you, just as a precaution."

"Surely, the danger has passed," the duke said. "We can send the man back to Brockton."

"Not yet," Maeve said. "There is more to this business than meets the eye. I am convinced of that."

JUST AS BRIANNA thought, Anna was in tears when she arrived.

"I cannot believe such a thing has happened. James is a calm, reasonable man. He would not murder anyone in cold blood. It is impossible!" Anna tore at her handkerchief.

"I do not believe it either. The Runners have made a mistake. I will see what can be done to affect his release."

"I know nothing of the law," Anna said.

"I think my brother can help us. Maeve will persuade him. She is wise. We will consult her."

"Oh, if only you can help!" Anna was crying again. "I have lost my husband. I cannot lose my only child as well."

Brianna was stricken. She felt this was her fault. The Winthrops had shown her nothing but kindness. Now they were suffering because of her.

"Come with me right now. We will talk to my brother. It will be all right." Brianna placed a comforting arm around Anna Winthrop.

They spoke very little during the coach ride. Brianna had not brought Gwen but Mrs. Winthrop, always a stickler for propriety, had her maid along with them. Clearly, Anna did not wish to say anything that could be gossiped about later in the servants' quarters.

Brianna found Maeve in the garden sitting at the gazebo at the center. She was at work creating a garland of white roses.

"I have been expecting you both," Maeve said, looking up.

Anna Winthrop looked surprised. Brianna was not. Maeve simply knew things; she sensed what others did not.

"Let us make haste to see Adam. He has been in his study since you left, Brianna. He sent for Prichard who is with him now."

"Will he mind us entering his domain?" Anna Winthrop asked. She looked hesitant.

"It will benefit your son that we see His Grace immediately," Maeve said, leading the way. Nevertheless, Maeve knocked before entering.

The duke called out: "Come in."

Brianna was aware instantly that this was a man's domain. The room smelled of leather, cigars and alcohol. Mr. Pritchard studied the three women in front of him, bowing politely. They reciprocated with curtsies. Pritchard was a tall man and thin as a rake. He had a prominent nose and a sharp chin as well as dark intelligent eyes.

The duke sat behind his large mahogany desk, long, well-manicured fingers steepled, an imposing figure.

"Mr. Pritchard has already engaged my solicitor for your son's case, Mrs. Winthrop. If it becomes necessary, we will also arrange for a first-rate barrister as well.'

"Thank you, Your Grace," Mrs. Winthrop said, her eyes lowered.

"No thanks necessary. I know how fond my sister is of you and your son and how good you have been to her. She reminds me incessantly." He turned an indulgent smile in Brianna's direction. "Peers of the realm such as myself can claim privilege of avoiding arrest in civil matters but not criminal. Still, a pity your son is not of the aristocracy. It would prove helpful."

"Peers and peeresses can plead privilege of peerage if convicted of a crime that was their first offense," Pritchard said. "However, that is not the case in murder or treason. They are grave offenses. So even for His Grace using his influence, this matter will not be easily resolved."

The duke gave his man of affairs a cautioning look. "We shall do our best. Rest assured."

Pritchard led them out of the duke's study.

Brianna turned to him. "Where is James being held?"

Pritchard hesitated "Newgate Prison."

Brianna was furious. "How dare they! He has not been found guilty."

Anna Winthrop virtually collapsed in her arms, weeping uncontrollably.

"Ladies, please," Pritchard said. "He will get his day in court."

"Can you not arrange for his release until then? He is not a common criminal but a prosperous businessman. I will see the magistrate myself if necessary."

"Most inappropriate, Lady Brianna. I will arrange his release."

"Whatever the bond may be, I will pay it," Mrs. Winthrop said.

"The duke has volunteered to arrange for bail," Pritchard informed her. "Your son has not yet had to appear for indictment in court. So we will obtain a release for the time being. Go home for now."

"I would like to visit my son and see to providing him with whatever he needs," Mrs. Winthrop said, her expression mulish.

Pritchard shook his head. "That is inadvisable. Prison is no place for a lady. I will see to his needs for you."

Maeve joined them. "I believe we could all use a fortifying cup of tea," she said, gently leading Brianna and Anna into the sitting room.

After they were seated and the tea rung for, Maeve looked thoughtfully at each of them.

"Since we do not believe James killed Mr. Foxworth, I think it is important to consider who might be guilty of such a crime. I do not believe the Runners will make the effort to further their investigation. They are good men to be sure but not insightful. As far as they are concerned, they have their murderer and will present their evidence at the Old Bailey at the appropriate time."

Brianna was horrified. "Surely, there must be something we can do. "

Maeve nodded. "I believe we must consider who might have a grievance with Mr. Foxworth."

"Assuming it was on my behalf," Brianna amended.

Maeve folded her hands together. She seemed lost in thought. "Perhaps. I suppose we should begin with that assumption."

"I will speak with those gentlemen who have expressed concern for me due to the threat that evil man presented toward me."

"Is that wise?" Mrs. Winthrop asked.

"Who else is there?" Brianna said.

"I could do it," Maeve replied.

Brianna shook her head so vehemently that some of the pins which held her hair in place fell out. "It is dangerous for you. You will soon be having your child. Besides, this trouble began with me. It is only appropriate that I see to discovering the truth."

"All right," Maeve said after giving it some thought, "but you must promise to be very careful. It is an undertaking that requires a certain amount of discretion and dare I say it, diplomacy."

"Her Grace is correct, my dear," Anna said. "Do be cautious in how you approach the gentlemen."

"Of course, I promise to do so."

No, it would not be easy. Who should she talk with and what should she say? She must give the matter some thought.

CHAPTER THIRTY-THREE

BRIANNA ASKED MAEVE TO EXTEND a dinner invitation to Charles and Caroline for the following evening. Maeve did so without comment or questions. Brianna was relieved when they received a note back that the young couple would be coming.

She was nervous about talking with them on such a delicate subject, but Maeve reassured her. "I will arrange that you speak with Charles privately. He is not a sensitive soul. Do not fear that you will insult him."

Brianna was not so certain of that. Maeve was like a sister to him, but she was not. She was on edge during dinner and spoke little. Charles and Caroline were in good spirits and took up most of the slack in the conversation.

The duke carved slices of beef but took none for himself.

"I thought that was your favorite," Maeve said.

"True. However, I lunched with Rundwall at White's today. We chose roast beef. You must join us there, Charles, one day soon, a most convivial atmosphere I assure you."

"I was with my other father today," Charles responded.

"I do not see Brockton dining at White's," the duke said.

"I wanted him to know that Caroline and I are going to have a child." Charles leaned over and kissed his wife.

"We thought so some months ago, but it proved to be not so. I announced it too soon. A mistake. This time, we are certain." Caroline smiled widely.

"I am delighted for both of you." Maeve's moonbeam eyes lit up with pleasure.

"Is it not wonderful!" Caroline exclaimed. "Maeve, our children will be able to play together."

Brianna wished them both happy as well. But how could she now ask Charles if he had any contact with Dirk Foxworth? It was unthinkable. The situation grew more difficult and complicated by the moment.

Regardless, it proved impossible to obtain a private word with Charles. After having trifle for dessert, Caroline announced that she was feeling very tired. Charles, as a concerned husband, insisted that they must leave early.

Brianna felt a sense of frustration. She shared her feelings with Maeve in private later.

"I do not think Charles is responsible for killing that dreadful man," Maeve said.

Brianna did not feel as certain. "Do you not think your feelings are influenced by the fact that you and Charles were like brother and sister?"

Maeve leaned toward her. "Perhaps. However, because of our close relationship, I believe I know his character better than anyone else would. Yes, Charles has a temper. He can become violent at times. As Mr. Brockton's debt collector, he did have something of a reputation. Other men feared him, it is true. However, Charles used his fists. He would not be sneaky. He confronted his adversaries. He would not attack another in the manner described by the Runners."

Brianna was still not convinced, but she chose not to disagree with Maeve. She went to bed that night considering what Maeve had said and wondering if her sister-in-law was right about Charles. She slept poorly. There were dreams, frightening ones, in which Dirk Foxworth was attacking her again.

"You will never be free of me," he whispered, digging his dagger into her throat.

She woke with a start. It was the middle of the night and still dark out. Wispy clouds moved over the face of the moon. She shivered. Brianna resolved she must visit James at the prison in the morning. She needed to see him.

BRIANNA LEFT IN the early morning before Maeve and the duke had risen. She dressed plainly, a gray pelisse over a simple white dress. She walked several blocks before hailing a hackney. She chose not to engage Ralph and the ducal coach. She did not wish to have anyone dissuade her.

The first thing she noticed about Newgate was the terrible stench. In her entire life, she had never smelled such an odor so foul. She took a handkerchief from her pocket and held it against her nose.

She was soon met by a guard who looked at her with some surprise.

"What you doin' here?" he said

"I have come to see Mr. James Winthrop."

"He ain't allowed no visitors." The man coughed and spat on the floor.

"Please, just for a moment. I am his sister. My mother needs to know that he is all right." She pressed some coins into his callused hand.

He shrugged. "Just for a minute then. No more."

She was relieved that her pleading and small bribe had worked. The guard led her through the prison which was dirty and squalid.

"Why do the floors crunch as we walk?" she asked.

"Due to the vermin, Miss, all of them lice and bedbugs."

Brianna cringed. She was relieved when the jailer finally brought her to the cell where James paced. He looked upset when he caught sight of her.

"What are you doing here?"

"I wanted to tell you myself that my brother is arranging your bond. He has a great deal of influence. You should be out of here shortly."

"Thank God!"

She reached out to him. He placed his hand to hers at the bars. They touched. She felt overcome with emotion.

"James, you did not kill that horrible man, did you?"

"I did not." His expression was earnest.

"I knew it could not be true. Maeve will help. We will find the real murderer."

"I do not want you putting your life in danger. There must be another way."

Brianna shook her head. "I do not think so."

The guard returned. Their private moment was over. There was so much more she had wanted to say to him. She wanted to tell him that she loved him. It was in her heart to do so. But ladies did not declare their feelings. It was not proper. It was against the rules of society. *Perhaps the rules should be changed,* she thought.

~♥~

JAMES COULD NOT believe that Brianna had risked visiting him in prison. How brave she was! He would have loved to take her into his arms and kiss her all over. She was not only beautiful but kind and generous. He almost wished he had killed Foxworth on her behalf. But someone else had done the deed. He did not fancy a noose around his neck for a crime he did not commit.

The guard who had brought Brianna to him returned later. "You are a lucky fellow," he said. "That young girl seemed right sweet on you. Claimed she was your sister, but I knew better. Still, she slipped me some coin to look the other way. You are lucky all right." He laughed through yellowed teeth.

"I do not feel lucky confined to a cell," he answered.

"They say you'll be getting out for a time soon. Got some friends in high places, don't you? Well, you might just end up hanging anyway." The man laughed again. It was an ugly sound.

James suddenly felt his neckcloth tighten. He wished to leave Newgate and never return.

CHAPTER THIRTY-FOUR

The following day, His Grace sent for Brianna in the early afternoon. Ellis led her into her brother's study where he appeared to be hard at work going over papers with Mr. Pritchard. He looked up as she entered the room.

"Pritchard informs me that Winthrop is now back home. Bail was set."

"That is splendid news," Brianna said. She smiled at her brother. "Thank you."

"Do not be overcome with joy yet. He will face an indictment in a matter of days," the duke cautioned.

"Perhaps by then the real killer will be discovered," Brianna responded.

"We cannot count on it. There was strong evidence."

"Merely circumstantial." She wanted to tell her brother that she had seen James, and he solemnly swore he did not murder Foxworth. But she realized that would cause a problem. If her brother knew she had gone to the prison to visit James, he would find a way to restrict her movements. So, she kept silent.

"I spoke with your friend," Pritchard said. "Although he has his own solicitor, it is only a fellow who he engages to draw up contracts, civil work. His Grace and I have obtained the services of an excellent barrister should it become necessary to go forward with a trial."

Brianna felt a sudden chill. "I do hope it does not come to that."

"We all feel the same," her brother said solemnly.

She left her brother to his paperwork. She was lost in thought. What should she do? How could she help James? She sought out Maeve. Talking to her sister-in-law always helped.

She found Maeve in the garden enjoying the sunshine.

"It is such a lovely day," Maeve said. She looked vividly fresh and alive dressed in a rose afternoon dress with a matching bolero jacket. Brianna wore a simple pink pastel with embroidered tulips across the hem. She observed they were both appropriately dressed for the garden.

"You have come to talk about your friend?"

"Yes, that is right." Should she confide in Maeve? She would. "I want to visit James and Anna today. I wish to discuss what happened."

"Take our coach and have Ralph accompany you. I am sorry I cannot go with you as well. But it will be well to take Gwen. You should have your maid along."

Brianna nodded. As usual, Maeve offered sensible counsel. "Make certain to wear my mother's necklace wherever you go," Maeve cautioned, then furrowed her brow.

Brianna took her sister-in-law's hand in her own. "I will do as you say."

Maeve smiled, clearly pleased.

On the short drive to the Winthrop residence, Brianna considered what she might say. She realized that it was imperative she know what exactly had happened and why James was arrested.

She and Gwen were led into the drawing room. Anna Winthrop soon appeared. Brianna told Gwen she could go out to the kitchen. "Do have a bite to eat," she said. "The Winthrop's cook is a wonderful baker. There are always fine pastries to feast on."

"A lovely compliment," Anna said. Brianna could see she was much more composed than the last time they saw each other.

Gwen hurried off toward the kitchen with enthusiasm. Brianna was glad to see her leave. She wanted her conversation with James and Anna to be private.

"Where is James?" she asked.

"Washing off the stench of the prison," Anna replied.

"Yes, it was horrible."

"He told me how you visited him there. It was so brave of you."

"Not at all," she denied. "I owe him that and much more."

Anna offered to serve tea, but Brianna declined. She waited nervously for James to join them. It seemed forever. Finally, he entered the room looking much better than he had the last time she saw him. He turned from his mother to Brianna. His eyes brightened.

"So wonderful to be here with both of you," he said.

"We feel the same way," his mother responded. "Let us sit down together."

"I know my brother is helping you," Brianna said. "However, I want to help you as well. I feel to blame for what happened to you."

James sat down beside her on the settee. "No, it was not your fault. Do not even think it." James leaned forward placing his head in his hands. "I should not have sought Foxworth at his establishment. It was foolish. I blame myself."

"What happened?" Brianna asked.

"You do not need to know."

She took his hands in hers. "I think I must know."

He looked up and their eyes met. "Very well. I confronted him and he threatened me."

"Louise, the madam of that house of ill repute, told us to take it outside. I refused at first, but Foxworth threw a blow at me. I was furious. Madam Louise pointed to an exit which turned out to be the alley at the side of the building. Foxworth followed me. He said some nasty things that I refuse to repeat in front of you and my mother. I told him never to go near you again. He pulled a dagger from a sheath in his boot and started toward me. I managed to knock it out of his hand and then I punched him. He went down and hit his head on the ground. I am certain he was not dead, merely momentarily stunned. He was definitely breathing. In any case, I realized it had been a mistake for me to try and deal with him. I left him there and quickly proceeded out of the alley."

"You told all of this to the Runners?"

"I did indeed," he affirmed.

"It is incredible that they did not believe you," Mrs. Winthrop said, her tone aggrieved.

"An injustice to be sure," Brianna agreed. "We will get this all sorted out." She tried to sound more reassuring than she felt.

"I do hope so," Anna said worriedly.

"Surely, a man like Foxworth must have had many enemies."

"The madam told the Runners that I was the last person to see him alive."

"We know she was wrong." She squeezed his hand. "Do not lose hope. We will discover the truth." But she realized the madam's testimony if given would be damaging in a trial.

Before she left, Brianna hugged Anna and then James. Truly, she loved them both and resolved to do everything she could to help James. Ralph was waiting outside the ducal coach when Brianna returned. His hands were folded over his broad expanse of chest. His expression was one of concern. He was unlikely to be a man that anyone would argue with, in her opinion.

"Ready to go home, Miss?" Ralph asked.

"Yes, I am." She looked up at Ralph. "Do you or Mr. Brockton know anything about Foxworth? I ask only because I want to help James. I am certain he did not kill that man."

Ralph nodded and rubbed his chin. "Mr. Brockton may run a gambling establishment, but he had no business with the likes of Foxworth. As for me, well, I tried my best to keep our Maeve away. That was when we were searching for you. After what Apple—Doris I mean—told her, Maeve made her mind up to find out about Foxworth. She thought he might be holding you. But she discovered that weren't true and so that was the end of it. She might not want to tell you about that though."

Brianna decided to be blunt. "Would you have killed Foxworth for what he tried to do?" she asked.

Ralph looked at her directly, their eyes meeting. "Miss, I could have easily squashed him like the cockroach he was, but I didn't do it. His Greatness said the law would handle matters and we was not to seek justice ourselves. I do things the right way."

Brianna could see from Ralph's expression that she managed to offend him. She regretted that, but as far as she was concerned, the question had to be asked. She turned and a footman helped her into the coach. A few minutes passed before she was joined by her maid.

"Oh, Lady Bri, I'm that sorry, I am. Didn't mean to make you have to wait for me." Gwen was breathing hard as if she had been running. Her cheeks were pink.

"Perfectly all right. I have only been out here a few minutes." Brianna wondered if Gwen had been flirting with one of the footmen. It seemed likely.

She spoke very little on the drive back to her brother's residence, thinking over the little she had learned in talking with both James and Ralph. She was missing information that might prove helpful—but what—and who to ask?

CHAPTER THIRTY-FIVE

BRIANNA HAD SOME QUESTIONS IN her mind when Lord Randall visited the following afternoon in the drawing room. As usual, he was pleasant and had brought flowers. He exchanged polite conversation with Maeve. She eventually offered a smile to each of them and announced that she was feeling tired and intended to take a nap.

"I will send your maid in, of course." Maeve rose, straightened her skirt, and left them.

"Would you like to take a walk or a ride?" Lord Randall said. He immediately moved to the settee to sit beside her.

Brianna moved over to allow some space between them. "At the moment, I am much concerned about James Winthrop and what will happen to him."

Lord Randall raised his brows. "I see," was all he said.

Her maid entered the room and seated herself on a straight back chair some distance from them discreetly allowing a measure of privacy.

"He visited that establishment of ill repute and gave Foxworth a warning. They engaged in an argument which turned physical. They ended up in the alley where Foxworth was later found dead."

"A serious error on your friend's part, I am afraid. Your brother had the authorities handling the matter. Winthrop should never have involved himself. Why did he?" Lord Randall gave her a sharp look.

Brianna turned away. “He was concerned for me. But I have spoken to James, and he swears he did not kill that wretched man.”

Lord Randall rose to his feet. “Your brother spoke to me of the arrest. He intends to help Winthrop as much as possible, and Adam does have considerable influence. However, murder is a grievous offense.” He began pacing the room, his hands behind his back. “Was there something you wish me to do as well?”

Brianna bit her lower lip. “On the evening we visited the theatre, you seemed to know who those disreputable ladies were.”

“The Cyprians? Yes, I daresay a great many gentlemen are acquainted with them on some level.”

“Are you acquainted with the brothel in question as well?”

Lord Randall turned and met her gaze directly with his own. “Are you accusing me, my dear?”

Brianna felt her cheeks flush. “Not precisely, no, but I thought you might have some knowledge that could be useful.”

“I do not.” His tone was suddenly clipped and angry. “Perhaps today is not a good one for us to take an excursion outdoors together. I will call again another time.”

He left abruptly. Brianna felt like crying. So far, she had managed to offend both Ralph and Lord Randall. She did not mean to insult or alienate either of them, only to learn the truth of what happened to Foxworth. Diplomacy was obviously not her forte. The worst part was she had learned nothing new from either one of them. Perhaps there was nothing new to be learned. She decided to discuss the matter with Maeve.

Brianna walked up the central hallway stairs and approached Maeve’s private quarters. Cautiously, she knocked gently on the door, not wishing to disturb Maeve if she was napping or if her brother happened to be there.

But Maeve called out for her to enter. Brianna found her sister-in-law seated at her desk writing a letter.

“If you are busy, I can come back later.”

Maeve shook her head, glossy black curls escaping their pins. “No, it is quite all right. This can wait. You wish to talk with me?”

Brianna nodded.

“Take a chair and sit beside me. Shall I send for tea?”

"No, thank you."

"You are concerned about your friend, Mr. Winthrop, I take it."

"I suppose that is obvious." She raised her eyes. "Maeve, I know he is innocent. He told me precisely what happened. He had punched that dreadful man in the face causing Foxworth to fall and be unconscious. Then he left. Someone else obviously hated Foxworth and saw an opportunity to kill him. James did not hit him with a large rock and fracture his skull, nor did he stab Foxworth in the back. James is not a murderer. I know he is not!"

"I know you believe that. I tend to agree with you, dear." Maeve spoke in a gentle, soothing tone of voice.

"I am afraid I have made a muddle of matters, however. I spoke to Ralph, thinking he might have accosted Foxworth."

"I do not believe Ralph would do such a thing. I have known him a very long time and he always fights fairly."

"I did offend him, and I am sorry." Brianna lowered her eyes. "I am afraid I did exactly the same thing with Lord Randall just now."

"Oh, dear, did you accuse him?" Maeve asked in a concerned voice.

Brianna nodded, unable to swallow the lump in her throat. "I did not directly accuse him, but I did mention he had pointed out to me that certain ladies in an opposite theatre box should not be acknowledged. He knew exactly who they were. In my naivete, I did not know. I considered that he might be acquainted with Foxworth and have a personal grudge beyond my situation."

Maeve tapped her feather quill thoughtfully. "How did he react to that accusation?"

"He was angry, more so than Ralph. I do not know if he will ever speak to me again."

Maeve took her hand. "My dear, he is your brother's best friend, and he does have a tender regard for you. He is also quite a good-natured fellow. He will forgive you." Maeve was thoughtful for a time. "There is something you must understand. A gentleman does not go about stabbing people in the back, especially if they are lying unconscious. Consider that it is an act of a coward. No gentleman wishes to ever be accused of such a thing. Do you comprehend that?"

Brianna gave a quick nod.

"Your brother once called a man out who besmirched my reputation."

Brianna's eyes widened. "Did he fight a duel over your honor?"

Maeve shook her head. "It turned out not to be necessary. Your brother has a reputation as a crack marksman and a superior swordsman. The other man left for the continent on the first available boat."

Brianna laughed despite herself.

"I will share with you some of my own history, although I rarely do so. When you disappeared and we had you searched for in vain, Doris gave us the information that Foxworth might have you. I decided to take matters into my own hands. It was reckless, but I found out where the brothel was located, and I entered planning to look for you. I was snatched up. If it were not for Adam coming after me, I shudder to think what might have happened, and all for naught at that. You were not there. You see now why the Runners should be the ones to investigate? Not you."

"Yes, but…"

Maeve raised her hand. "Please listen to me. Ask no more questions which may alienate others. I will tell you that neither Ralph nor Howard would ever murder another person in such a cowardly manner—neither would your brother."

A thought occurred to her. "Maeve, what about Charles? I know he is now an aristocrat, but he was not brought up as one. You know that better than anyone. He seems proud of the fact that he served as Mr. Brockton's enforcement agent in collecting gambling debts."

"Charles might be capable of beating a man to death. He can be a fearsome adversary. I will grant you that. However, he would face another in direct combat. There is nothing sneaky about him." Maeve frowned at her, clearly aggrieved.

"I apologize for being accusatory. I do not mean to be unjust. But, Maeve, the Runners feel they have their murderer. I owe James and Anna Winthrop a great deal. I might be dead myself if it were not for them. They are kind and generous people. I feel it incumbent upon me to do everything I can to be of help to them."

"And you have strong emotions connected with James Winthrop, do you not?" Maeve studied her knowingly.

Brianna nodded. "Yes, but I am not certain they are reciprocated. I am not endeavoring to ingratiate myself with him or his mother. I would like to think my motives are purer."

"Then we must think on this. Let us discuss the matter further later in the day. I do really feel the need for a respite now." Maeve pressed her hands against her stomach.

"I did not mean to tire you," Brianna said.

"You did not, but I do think better after I have rested."

Brianna left her sister-in-law, closing the door quietly behind her as Maeve lay down on her bed for her nap. She felt suddenly guilty for upsetting Maeve. Perhaps Maeve was right. The murderer could not be Charles, Ralph, or Lord Randall, and most certainly not her brother.

Possibly the person who murdered Dirk Foxworth was not someone she knew or even knew her. Maeve's analysis caused her thoughts to move in a different direction entirely. One thing was certain: time was running out for James. Soon he would be indicted and bound over for trial. The situation was desperate indeed. The hangman's noose was not far off. She shuddered at the thought.

CHAPTER THIRTY-SIX

THAT EVENING THEY DINED WITHOUT company. Brianna feared she had perhaps insulted the duke and duchess's friends and they were loath to visit. When Brianna mentioned it, Maeve assured her it was far from the truth.

"They are not a sensitive lot I can assure you," she said. "I simply thought we would have a quiet meal this evening, just the three of us."

Her brother nodded his agreement. "Life has been hectic of late. This suits me as well." He appeared to be in good spirits and Brianna was relieved. Hopefully, Lord Randall had not complained about her behavior toward him.

After a hearty dinner, the duke left Brianna and Maeve for a time to work in his study. They went to the drawing room.

"I fancy a cup of tea," Maeve said. "Would you like one as well?"

She agreed, and Maeve sent for tea.

"What shall we do for amusement?" Maeve questioned. "Would you like me to read your future? I can use tarot cards. I have a deck in the credenza."

"No, thank you. I do not believe in such things. I do not mean to insult you, however."

"You are not doing so," Maeve said. "Adam is not a believer either. But I have a certain ability to read the cards and see things through them. Perhaps we will use the tea leaves instead of the cards. Yes, that will suffice."

Brianna could hardly refuse. It would have been impolite. Maeve ordered boiled water and tea leaves to be brought separately with the tea service. Afterwards, she placed the tea leaves into a china cup and carefully poured hot water over them. When Maeve deemed the temperature to be right, she handed Brianna the cup.

"Drink," she said, "but you must leave a little of the liquid in the cup."

Brianna did as she was told. When she finished drinking the tea, Maeve took the cup from her. Holding the cup in her left hand, Maeve swirled the remaining contents around three times from left to right. Then slowly but carefully she inverted the cup over a saucer. Maeve left the cup upside down for a minute, afterwards rotating it three times. Finally, she turned the cup upright again, adjusting the handle to point south.

"Now we are ready to read the tea leaves and find out what advice can be obtained and perhaps you will learn something of your future."

Brianna peered inside the cup. Tea leaves were stuck inside in various shapes and clusters. *How could one find meaning in such things*, she wondered. But Maeve was intent on examining them. Suddenly, she looked up and frowned.

"The wings of the bird are here." Maeve pointed high on the inside of the cup. "They show that you will insist on your freedom. But the cross on the other side, that worries me. It symbolizes trouble ahead, that you will be in danger." Maeve took her hand and looked into Brianna's eyes. "You must promise me that you will be very careful."

"Of course, I am cautious."

Maeve shook her head. "I do not think so. Where is the necklace? Why are you not wearing it?"

Brianna touched her neck. "I left it upstairs in my room. I did not think to wear it this evening. I am perfectly safe here. Dirk Foxworth will not be bothering me again after all."

"That is true. But you must wear the necklace for protection until it is safe for you. The tea leaves do not lie. You are still in danger."

Brianna did not try to contradict Maeve. As a Gypsy, Maeve apparently was superstitious, believing she had some mystical psychic power. There was no question that Maeve had a strong temperament and personal presence, but Brianna remained dubious that the ability to read tea leaves could offer insight into a person's future.

~♥~

James thought about Brianna. He wanted to be with her. He felt desire—no it was more than desire. She was truly a golden girl, one of a kind. He shook his head. It was impossible to seek a relationship with her, no matter how much he might want it.

He chided himself about how foolish he had been to seek out Foxworth again. He meant only to warn the man off, but this time more strongly than before. He should have known better. There was no hope of dealing with that sort of fellow. Whoever had killed him did the world a great service. Ironic that he should be blamed. The last thing he wanted was to bring grief to his mother and Brianna. They both deserved better. His situation seemed hopeless.

His mother joined him in his father's library. She placed her arms around him.

"My dear boy, I cannot believe what is happening."

He patted her arm. "Neither can I. It does seem impossible. I always pride myself on being able to read people. I thought I could warn Foxworth off but that did not work out well at all. I must apologize to you, Mother, for bringing such added sorrow to your life."

She gave him a weary smile. "You have always been joy to my life and your father's."

Choked with emotion, he hugged her. He loved his mother and he realized he loved Brianna as well. It would be difficult leaving them both if it came to that. He felt pain in his heart.

"I am going to visit Brianna. Will you come with me?" he asked his mother.

She shook her head. "Not today. I believe you and she need some time alone together."

Brianna heard someone knocking at the front door and she came downstairs. Ellis opened the door. James entered and the butler took his hat and gloves. Brianna was glad to see him.

"Is Lady Brianna at home? I have come to see her," James said.

"I will announce you, sir, if you will remain here in the hall."

Brianna rushed the rest of the way down the stairs. "No need. I am here. So happy to see you, James. I wish to talk with you. Come into the garden with me where we may speak in private."

He took her arm, and they walked side by side. She did not speak again until they reached the gazebo in the heart of the shrubbery. Once they were seated, she turned to him with an earnest look.

"I believe I have an idea how we may learn what actually happened when Foxworth was killed."

James shook his head. "I do not want you involved in this any further. It is dangerous for you. I will not let you risk it."

Brianna raised her head. "You cannot stop me."

"Do not force me to bring the matter before your brother. He would doubtless lock you in your room until I am hanged."

She burst into tears, unable to hold back her emotions. "Do not talk of such a thing. You are the one in jeopardy, not I. You endangered yourself by trying to deal with Foxworth on my behalf. Something Maeve told me gave me an idea for a plan to find out the truth."

He viewed her sharply, narrowing his eyes. "What sort of a plan?"

"I prefer not to say."

He gave an exasperated sigh. "Little goose, you do not help me in this manner."

"Someone must do something."

"Promise me that whatever mad notion you might have concocted will be abandoned now at my request."

"I promise nothing." He could be infuriating. Her plan was his only hope. Why did he not realize that?

"I feel like shaking you," he said.

"Then do it." Why was she daring him? But her passion was stirred.

The next moment, James grabbed her, pulling her into his arms, kissing her with abandon born of a wild desperation. The kiss was not gentle. It was full of hunger and need. She kissed him back with the same urgency.

His hands roamed her body. She felt a strange tingling in the nipples of her breasts, a delightful tightening. Her hands mimicked his. She touched his face and then his chest. As his hands moved lower on her body, so did her hands on his. She wanted him in every way that men and women wanted each other. She did not question why, only that it was so. Finally, they separated, completely breathless.

He stood up abruptly. "Find someone else, some aristocrat worthy of you."

He left so quickly that she was shocked and without words. Did he not realize there was no other man for her?

~♥~

THE DUKE SOUGHT her out later in the day. She was playing a rendition of *Greensleeves* on the piano and did not notice that he stood listening for a time.

"Ellis informed me that Winthrop came to see you earlier."

She stopped playing and turned to her brother. "That is correct."

"It would probably be best if you did not entertain his company in the future."

She looked away from him. "I think under the circumstances it would be best not to discuss James further." She stood up, spine straight, and walked away from him.

When she saw Ellis, Brianna felt annoyed. What right did the butler have to spy on her, to tell her brother who she saw?

"Let my brother know I will be in my room for the rest of the day and evening. I do not wish to be disturbed by anyone."

"Yes, my lady," the elderly servant responded with an expressionless nod.

Brianna hurried up the stairs and went directly to her room. Beneath her mattress, she had collected various copies of newspapers from her brother's library. Now she sifted through *The Times, The Morning Chronicle, The Morning Herald* and *Morning Post* until she finally found the information she was searching for. She could hardly have asked anyone for the address of Foxworth's establishment where he had been murdered. Not only would they have been shocked, but someone could possibly have figured out her intentions. This was something she was resigned to carrying out by herself with no interference from anyone else.

CHAPTER THIRTY-SEVEN

THE FOLLOWING MORNING, BRIANNA LET Gwen know she was going to be busy writing letters all morning and did not wish to be disturbed. She then dressed in her oldest clothing, one of her gray school uniforms that made her look younger than she was. She combed her hair neatly but left it down, caught back by a plain white ribbon. She took her reticule and placed a portion of her earnings saved from her brief time working for the Winthrops inside it.

The difficult part was waiting near the backstairs to make certain none of the servants were about. When all was quiet, she slipped down the stairs and outside through the side door into the alleyway. From there she walked quickly down several streets. The sun was up, and the air was already warm. It promised to be another good day. She let out a sigh. Perhaps that boded well for her endeavor.

She hailed a hackney and gave the driver the address she had written down from the newspaper. He looked at her dubiously.

"Young lady, is you sure this is where you want to be going?"

"Yes, sir, I am quite certain."

He scratched the stubble on his chin. "You not be lookin' much older than my own girl. I wouldn't let her near that place."

"You are right," Brianna said consideringly, "please let me off a street away." She opened her purse. "I will pay you in advance."

That seemed to convince the driver. He did as she asked. As the coach traveled, she dug her fingernails into the palm of her hand. She was frightened yet certain. She was doing the only thing left, the only thing that made any sense.

JAMES FELT RIDICULOUS calling at Clarmont House at such an early hour. However, he felt it was necessary. He lifted the lion's head knocker and brought it down with a loud thud. It took two more tries before the door was answered. A footman in livery responded. James asked to be announced. He was told to wait in the hall. He anxiously walked back and forth on the gold and white inlaid marble floor. A few minutes passed and finally, the butler appeared.

"Sir, it is too early to call on either His Grace or Her Grace." The butler's manner was coldly aloof.

"I have not come to see either of them. I wish to talk with Lady Brianna. It is a matter of some urgency."

"Lady Brianna left instructions that she was not to be disturbed."

Was it as he feared? Was the girl up to something? She had more than hinted at it when they last spoke. It had not immediately occurred to him that she would do something reckless in an effort to save him from the gallows. But last night as he lay awake, he mulled over her last words to him.

"I believe I must speak with His Grace," James said.

The butler, old enough to be his grandfather, gave James a stern look. "Sir, this is not an appropriate time to call. Leave your card and I will inform His Grace."

Fortunately, at that moment the duke descended the central staircase. He raised a haughty brow. "Winthrop, what are you doing here?"

"I am concerned about Lady Brianna. I fear she might be attempting something foolhardy on my behalf."

Her Grace was not far behind her husband. She responded, "I believe Brianna is in her room." She turned to the butler. "Ellis, please inform Lady Brianna she is requested here now."

The butler nodded and went upstairs.

"Really, Winthrop, I do not appreciate you being here. I am sorry about your problems, but I fail to understand why you must behave in this dramatic manner." The duke's berating tone of voice was offensive.

James began to feel embarrassed. Perhaps he was wrong and had misinterpreted what Brianna had said to him. In the heat of passion, people said many things they should not have.

It seemed like forever before Ellis returned. He was followed by a young ginger-haired girl who James recalled was Brianna's maid.

"Lady Brianna isn't in her room," the girl said. "I don't know where she be."

The duke told both the maid and butler to look around the house for Brianna. No one had seen her this morning, they soon discovered. The duke was alarmed.

"Oh, dear, I believe I know where she might have gone to," the duchess said. "I told her something I should not have the other day and I think it put an idea in her head. But the situation can be remedied," she promised both her husband and James on seeing their concerned expressions. "Mr. Winthrop, you did the right thing coming here this morning."

"Shall I go look for her?" James asked.

The duchess shook her head. "No, that would just compound your problems. Leave this to me." She gave both himself and the duke a reassuring smile.

BRIANNA FOLLOWED THE street numbers. She let go of the breath she had been holding. From the outside, the brothel looked no different from any other building in the flower district, although it was set back from the street and there was an ornate iron gate at the front. The impression was neither shabby nor elegant. Brianna had no idea what to expect. She realized that despite her early life with her mother, she had been rather sheltered.

When she walked up the steps and knocked at the door, it was answered not by a butler but by a young woman dressed in a low-cut, revealing gown of a gauzy thin material. It was obvious she wore no form of undergarment. Her nipples were almost completely exposed. Brianna did her best not to appear shocked.

The girl looked her up and down. "Did you want something 'ere?"

Brianna cleared her throat. "Yes, I am looking for employment. Can you take me to whoever is in charge?"

The girl sneered at her. "What would the likes of you be doing 'ere?"

"I will discuss that with your employer," she said. Looking weak or frightened would accomplish nothing. She lifted her chin.

"Very well then, I takes you back to see Madam. Follow along."

Brianna followed the young woman into the hallway and found herself in a large, opulent room. There were statues placed about, white marble figures of men and women done in the Greek and Roman style. But the figures were presented in many forms of erotic congress, vividly graphic. Brianna was somewhat shocked by the indelicacy but reminded herself of where she had come. Heavy purple draperies were pulled to keep out the light of day. There was thick, plush purple carpeting and comfortable chairs and settees all around the room. One wall was mirrored, and she caught sight of herself in it. She thought how out of place she looked in such a room.

The girl led her down a narrow hallway to an office of sorts. An older woman sat behind a desk in what appeared to be a masculine-looking room. It smelled of stale cigars. The woman was on the fat side and wore heavy makeup. Her short, feather-cut hair was dyed a brassy red and she wore a damped-down bodice, which proved revealing of her well-endowed bosom.

"What does your kind want here, dearie?"

"She's asking for work." The young woman laughed as if this amused her.

"Mr. Foxworth told me if I ever needed employment I should come here," Brianna quickly interposed.

The older woman's eyes narrowed. "And when was that?"

"Several months ago. I was employed as a nanny at the time. He saw me in the park with the children and made the offer. I was recently let go without a character reference and am nearly destitute." Brianna lowered her eyes.

"You're asking for Mr. Foxworth?" the woman said as she eyed Brianna suspiciously.

"He told me I could find him here."

"You could have—if he was still around. Suppose you didn't know he was dead?"

Brianna attempted to look surprised, opening her mouth and eyes wide.

"You still want work here? You got any idea what kind of work that is, girl?"

She nodded.

"I'm in charge of everything now. Call me Madam Louise. Understood?"

Brianna gave another nod.

"What's your name, girl?"

Brianna thought quickly. "I'm Belle," she replied.

"That's a good name for one of our girls. I have to look you over first. If I don't approve, you're out the door. We got fancy gents for clientele here, not like at Foxworth's other houses. But I can see why he thought you'd fit. The aristos, they like innocent-looking girls like you that talk nice. I'll give you a tryout tonight. If you do well, I'll let you stay. The master at the home you was working at, I suppose he took a turn or two with you?" The woman had a guttural dirty laugh that chilled Brianna to the marrow of her bones. "Never mind. You don't have to answer. I hear the same story over and over. The girls who work here are treated very well indeed. This is not your usual establishment. A girl must be very good to remain. She must be of the best. You'll have to learn quick how to please our patrons." She turned to the girl who had led Brianna. "Nell, give her over to Fleur to get properly dressed and ready. Fleur will explain what this green girl needs to know."

"Yes, Madam Louise." Nell turned to Brianna. "Well, don't just stand there. Follow me."

Brianna did as she was told. The upstairs corridor held many rooms it seemed. One door was open, and a young dark-haired woman stood in front of a mirror combing her hair. She was dressed in a revealing translucent white gown. Nell called out to her.

"Louise says you got to take this girl on and tell her what's what."

Fleur looked her up and down. "I suppose she wants me to provide a gown for her too?"

"That's right. You earn enough. You can afford it. Looks like you and her are about the same size. She's all yours." Nell smirked and then quickly sashayed away.

Fleur took Brianna's arm and led her into the room. It was a well-appointed bedchamber. The first thing she noticed was the wall murals of nude male and female figures in classical design, arranged in a variety of erotic poses. In the center of the room was a large tester bed covered with a lush red velvet spread. The carpeting matched in color and luxury. It was gaudy and garish, yet the overall impression was sensual.

"Nice, ain't it?" Fleur said. "Nothing but the best for the customers here." She sounded bitter.

"Yes, I can see that."

"You been in the business long?" Fleur eyed her suspiciously.

"No, not long."

"Well, you're pretty and got nice melons." Fleur indicated Brianna's breasts. "That's what the men like. Rich or poor, they all want the same thing."

"I was told Mr. Foxworth died recently. He was the reason I came here."

Fleur raised her brows. "You knew him?"

"Yes, I was surprised to find out that he was dead. Did you know what happened to him?"

"Well, I'm not one to gossip, but a few of us saw it. Couldn't help it really. They was so loud."

"What occurred?" Brianna pressed.

Fleur sat down on her bed. "Come closer." She looked out into the hallway and then closed her door.

Brianna pulled over a rickety chair and sat down next to the bed where Fleur again settled herself. "This young man came, handsome he was, well-spoken and well-dressed. It was the middle of the day, and he insisted on seeing Foxworth. Well, Louise didn't like that one bit. She told him to get out. He refused, said he would not leave until Foxworth came out into the hall. He and Louise made quite a commotion I will tell you. Finally, Louise sent Nell to fetch Mr. Foxworth." Fleur paused, picking a bit of lint from her gown.

"What happened then?" Brianna urged.

"Well, the two men argued about some gel or other. The young fellow threatened Mr. Foxworth, told him to never bother this person again or there would be hell to pay. Foxworth told the fellow to get out, but he wouldn't move. Finally, Louise said they should settle the matter outside. We girls were upstairs but we ran to the windows so we could watch what happened next."

"What did occur?"

Fleur leaned forward. "They went out in the alleyway. Soon as they were out there, Mr. Foxworth pulled his dirk from his boot and tried to slash the young man. But the fellow moved real quick like for a cit, don't you know. Anyway, he smacked the knife from Mr. Foxworth's hand, and it fell to the ground."

Brianna leaned forward on the edge of the chair. "What occurred after that?"

Fleur smiled remembering. "The young man planted a facer on him, punched Mr. Foxworth hard and he went down on the ground. Then the fellow stormed off leaving Mr. Foxworth lying there. It was quite a sight, I will tell you. I almost cheered. Foxworth was a nasty piece of work. No one liked him, only feared him."

"Did you see what happened next?" Brianna asked.

Fleur looked around. Suddenly her voice was little more than a whisper. "I don't think I should say."

"Why not?"

"I don't want no trouble." Fleur looked uneasy, pale even though her face was made up heavily.

"You and any of the other girls should speak up."

Fleur shook her head. "No, it ain't possible. This is our livelihood. We can't afford to lose it. There's no other kind of work for the likes of us."

"But, Fleur, if you would come forward and tell the Runners what you know, you would save the life of James Winthrop. You already told me he left Foxworth alive. Do you know who committed the murder? Did you see?"

Fleur would only shake her head. "I can't say." Fleur narrowed her eyes. She appeared frightened. "Who are you? What are you really doing here?"

This was not going to be easy. Brianna decided to be forthright. "Fleur, my brother is a very important man. He would see to it that you are protected and taken care of if you tell the authorities what you know. I can promise you that."

Fleur stared at her suspiciously. "I repeat, who are you? I thought you wanted to be one of us. You're a sneak. You don't have good intentions and I ain't no snitch."

"It is not that way at all. You would be saving a man's life, one who is blameless. You already said you saw Mr. Foxworth quite alive when Mr. Winthrop left the premises. Could you not state that in court if it even comes to that?"

Fleur jumped up.

Brianna grabbed the older girl's arm. "You will be paid generously for your trouble. Come with me now. You do not have to be afraid. I promise you."

Fleur shook her head, hair flying around. "Madam Louise would find out. She's got a bad temper. No telling what she'd do to me." Her eyes were wide open.

Suddenly there was knocking at the door. "Here now, why's this door locked?"

It was Nell. Fleur hurried to open the door.

Nell eyed them both with suspicion out of the corner of her eye. "You doin' something you shouldn't be?"

"No, Nell. We was just talking, that's all."

Nell looked at them askance. "What were you talking about?"

"Nothing." Fleur folded her arms over her breasts.

"I don't like this new girl. I'm goin' to have a word with Louise about her."

"No, don't do that." Fleur grabbed Nell's arm.

"Don't you tell me what to do!"

Nell backhanded Fleur. The girls started fighting in earnest, pulling hair and slapping each other. Finally, Fleur grabbed a pitcher and hit Nell with it knocking the smaller woman to the floor unconscious. Fleur turned to Brianna.

"Now see what you made me do. You're a troublemaker, you are. Nell's gonna complain to Louise and I'll get a beating."

"Come with me. As I told you, all you need to do is tell the truth of what happened to Mr. Foxworth, and you'll be handsomely rewarded. The young man they are blaming is well-to-do. He will pay you and so will my brother."

Fleur stared at Nell. "All right, I'll come with you."

"Right now," Brianna implored. She grabbed Fleur's hand and pulled her toward the door.

"We best go the back way. Don't want to run into Louise or any of the other girls."

Fleur led the way. They were both breathless by the time they managed to reach the street. Brianna's heart was pounding, but she tried not to show how frightened she was. Dealing with Fleur it was necessary to appear confident.

"I will hail us a hackney," she said. But just as she stepped toward the street, the ducal coach pulled up. Brianna was astonished.

Ralph stepped down. "Ready to go home, Miss?"

"Yes, thank you. Ralph, how did you know where I had gone? I left no note."

He offered a wry smile. "Why Miss Maeve, of course. There's nothing she don't know. When they saw you had left, she said you would come here and sent me to fetch you." He turned to Fleur. "Who have we here?"

"This is Fleur. She is to be our guest. She will be the witness for Mr. Winthrop."

"Aye. Well, get yourselves into the coach, ladies, and we'll be on our way."

A young footman helped them enter, and they drove off quickly.

CHAPTER THIRTY-EIGHT

JAMES LET OUT A SIGH of relief when he saw Brianna enter the front hall. He had been pacing back and forth, his hands folded behind him.

"I was so worried about you," he said. He took Brianna in his arms and held her tightly before realizing what he had done and releasing her.

She smiled at him. "It is good to see you too," she said.

The duke strode into the hall. "My God, girl, have you no sense whatever, going off that way?"

Brianna curled her lower lip. "No one else was going to do it. Someone needed to help James."

"You should be whipped," the duke countered.

"How dare you! I did what was right. James only went to that horrible place to deal with Foxworth on my behalf. I felt the only place to find out what actually happened was to go to the source."

"I understand," Maeve said, entering the hall. "But you should have at least let me know what you were about."

"And have you stop me? No, I think not." Brianna raised her chin.

"She's a brave lass just like our duchess," the man standing behind Brianna said.

"Thank you, Ralph, for bringing our Bri back safe and sound," the duchess said, turning to the stalwart man who pulled his forelock in a gesture of respect.

James had not noticed the man's presence until this moment. James now became aware of the young woman who stood beside Ralph, as did the duke and duchess.

"Brianna, who is this person?" the duke asked.

"My name is Fleur, sir. Your sister brought me here."

"Fleur is a witness to what happened to Mr. Foxworth. She saw the encounter from the window in her room. Other girls saw it as well, but I only got to talk with Fleur before we were forced to leave the premises."

"Why do we not all go into the drawing room. I will ring for refreshments. Then we may discuss this matter in some detail and in comfort," the duchess suggested.

Everyone was agreeable. After they were seated, Brianna began to tell them what had transpired that morning.

"You took a terrible risk," her brother said in a stern voice.

Brianna shrugged. "I felt it was necessary."

"I wouldn't have you do such a thing for my sake," James said, his expression earnest.

"How could I not?"

She gave him a speaking look. It was all he could do not to take her in his arms and kiss her thoroughly. But he reminded himself where he was and how unseemly such thoughts were when he did not intend to offer for her.

"Fleur, is it? What have you told my sister that will matter in court?" The duke was all business as he brought them back to the question at hand.

Fleur fluffed her hair the way a bird might fluff its feathers. "Well, guv, you see as I told your sister, several of us ran to the windows upstairs when we heard the commotion and Louise ordered the men outside. We knew there was going to be a fight. Naturally, we was game to see it all."

"And what exactly happened?" the duke demanded.

"They went out into the alleyway. Mr. Foxworth, he started pulling his knife from his boot. Well, this young man clobbered Mr. Foxworth before he could be stabbed. Self-defense it was plain and simple."

The duke stood and walked closer to Fleur. He pointed to James. "Did this fellow hit Foxworth on the head with a heavy rock while he was on the ground?"

Fleur shook her head. "No, sir, he did not." She folded her arms across her chest.

"Did he stab Foxworth in the back with the man's own dagger?"

"No, he did not." Her voice was clear and firm.

James was relieved to hear her speak those words. Brianna had truly brought a witness that could save him. It was remarkable.

"And will you swear to this in a court of law?" The duke's tone of voice was just as firm.

Fleur nodded. "Yes, but the young lady here, she said I was to be repaid." She waited anxiously for the duke to respond.

The duke turned on Brianna with a sharp look. "I am certain she meant in a manner of speaking."

"Well, this palace you folks lives in tells me you got plenty of blunt. You're probably rich as Croesus, ain't you?"

James groaned inwardly. This girl was shrewd. She was not about to give anything away for free.

"Let me explain something to you, young woman," the duke said in his superior manner, "in court, you will be asked if you have been paid for your testimony. You cannot lie. That would be perjury. You can be jailed for that. Giving false testimony in the case of a capital crime is a serious offense. Do you understand?"

Fleur nodded but did not offer a response. She looked down at her slippers.

"We will have you stay with us for the time being, at least until Mr. Winthrop's case is settled. Then we will talk further."

"My clothes, all my things are in my room back at the house," Fleur said. She looked stricken. The seriousness of what she had done caught up with her. "I can't go back there. Louise would whip me. She's a mean one."

The duchess rose. "Fleur, we will find some lovely clothes for you to wear. I believe you are close to Brianna's size. She will let you choose some appropriate garments. I will have our housekeeper find you a suitable room. I can assure you that I have helped many girls start new and better lives and you will find yourself in a much better position in the future." Unlike the duke, his wife spoke in a calming, soothing manner.

The duchess rang for her housekeeper, a lean, no-nonsense sort of woman.

"Mrs. Dunne, this is Fleur. She will be our guest for a time. Please take her upstairs and settle her in a suitable accommodation. Make her comfortable. Send Gwen to her."

"Come with me, girl," Mrs. Dunne said. Fleur responded to that voice of authority and followed her out of the room.

The duke turned to the burly man they called Ralph. "Do keep an eye out for Fleur just in case she changes her mind and decides to bolt. If she does, bring her back. We need her in court tomorrow."

Ralph nodded and left them.

The duke then turned to James. "I will be with you tomorrow. So will the barrister we engaged. If Fleur does not recant, we shall have you free by the afternoon."

James released a shaky breath. "Thank you, Your Grace."

"No thanks necessary, young man, we are not on safe ground as yet. And I am not doing this for your sake. I realize you were only trying to protect Brianna, no matter how misguided your efforts."

James lowered his eyes in embarrassment. What must Brianna think of him? But when he dared to look up, he saw that she was looking at him with admiration, her eyes bright with what he interrupted as affection. At that moment, he felt it had all been worth it.

"May I come tomorrow and sit in the gallery?" Brianna asked. It was clear to him that he mattered to her.

"No, you may not," the duke said. "Women are not welcome unless they are witnesses."

"I believe you are being arbitrary," Brianna said. She did not seem the least bit afraid of her brother. James admired her courage in standing up to the duke. The man was an imposing figure.

For Brianna's sake as much as for his own, he made an effort to appear confident, but in truth, he cursed himself for a fool. The duke was right. The Runners would have taken Foxworth into custody had he not gotten himself involved. What was wrong with him? He never behaved in such an ill-considered manner. He was rational and sensible, but he conceded, not where Brianna was concerned.

CHAPTER THIRTY-NINE

BRIANNA WAITED IMPATIENTLY, WONDERING WHAT was happening in court. Had her brother and the barrister he had chosen been successful in obtaining the release of James? Did Fleur's eyewitness testimony sway the Runners or the judge?

The clock in the drawing room chimed at noon. Surely the duke would return soon. Maeve entered the room. She wore a floral print sack dress which hardly disguised her increasing stomach.

"There you are," she said pleasantly. Maeve conferred a sunny smile on her. "Do not be fearful. I am certain all will go well for Mr. Winthrop today."

"It is so frustrating. I wish I could have been there." She took a turn around the room.

'Do not fuss. All will be fine."

Brianna turned to Maeve. "I do not see how you can be certain of such a thing. So much could go wrong."

"My intuition is rarely faulty."

Brianna could only hope that Maeve was right. However, she had to concede that Maeve was rarely wrong. Perhaps there was such a thing as second sight after all.

Her brother returned at two o'clock in a good mood. "Success!" he exclaimed. "Brianna, your protector is once again a free man."

She peeked behind the duke.

"No, he is not here. We left him at his home. Doubtless, his mother was in the throes of agony waiting to find out what would become of her son. You look disappointed."

"No, I am not. Anna deserves to know what has happened."

"It went well." The duke turned to his wife. "You and Brianna dressed Fleur perfectly. She looked like a virginal angel in that high-necked white gown. Her testimony did the trick."

"Where is she?" Maeve asked.

"I believe she went to the kitchen. She wanted to tell some of the staff of her adventure. Those are her sort of people."

"Yes, I am aware she feels comfortable with them," Maeve agreed.

"What will happen to her now?" Brianna asked.

"A good question," the duke said.

"I have a feeling matters will work out well for her," Maeve said.

"You and your intuition," the duke said fondly, bestowing a kiss on his wife's forehead.

"For the time being, she should stay with us," Maeve said. Her expression was distant as if her thoughts were far away. "I believe she likely saw the murder take place but did not wish to inform."

"Why is that?" Brianna questioned. She was somewhat bewildered.

The duke exchanged a look with his wife. "The murderer may well be someone she knows and fears."

Maeve nodded. "I think that is so. She definitely fears this person. By keeping silent Fleur probably mistakenly believes she is safe."

"But you do not think that is so," Brianna surmised.

"No, this person may come looking for Fleur, especially since she was the witness for Winthrop today," her brother said.

"That is why we must keep her here for now," Maeve said. "She deserves our protection."

BRIANNA CONSIDERED THE conversation she had with her brother and Maeve for several days afterwards. She did her best to spend time with Fleur. But the young woman was restless.

"When will I get my pay?" Fleur asked.

"Soon," Brianna replied.

"Well, I would like new clothes in the meantime. I need to shop. Your things are dull. They don't do a thing for me."

"I will ask Ralph to drive us in a few days," Brianna said. She doubted that Maeve or her brother would approve, but Fleur was becoming irritable. There was no purpose in pointing out to her that staying within the walls of the ducal mansion was to her benefit. Fleur was not the most sensible of women.

Brianna was feeling restless herself. James had not visited. Perhaps she would never see him again. The thought depressed her. Maeve seemed to understand her feelings and spoke to her sympathetically.

"You must not pine away for Mr. Winthrop, my dear." Maeve gently sat Brianna down beside her in the gazebo on a sunny afternoon in late August.

"I have feelings for him," she said.

"Yes, I realize that. But it is incumbent upon him to address the matter. I observe he has feelings for you as well. However, he has not proposed, has he?"

Brianna shook her head.

"I know this has made you sad, but you cannot force the issue. Something is holding him back. He obviously does not wish to discuss it."

"What if I were to propose marriage to him?"

"Oh, my dear, it simply is not done."

"Did you not suggest marriage to my brother?"

Maeve smiled and shook her head. "I led your brother a merry chase until he insisted upon marriage. Of course, he wanted me for a mistress at first, but I refused. He was a dreadful rake."

Brianna looked up at Maeve in surprise. "My brother, a rake?"

Maeve smiled and nodded.

"I cannot imagine it. He seems so stuffy."

"Not when we are alone, I can assure you." Maeve laughed. "Perhaps Mr. Winthrop needs to see you pursued by other gentlemen."

"Would not that cause him to lose interest in me entirely?"

Maeve straightened her skirt. "No, I believe he would be jealous and want you even more. When the time is right, you will have a fine come-out. We will plan a magnificent ball for the occasion. There will be many interested gentlemen."

Brianna shook her head. "I have already told you and my brother such things do not interest me."

"You deserve to have a husband of your own and a good life. Living here will only be temporary," Maeve said.

Maeve seemed so certain of her future. Brianna wished she could be as well.

CHAPTER FORTY

As August turned into September, Maeve went into labor on a rainy late summer day which no longer seemed like summer at all. When Brianna knocked at Maeve's door that morning, she found her sister-in-law pacing around her bedroom occasionally moaning.

"What is it? What is wrong?" Brianna asked in alarm.

"It is the child. It is coming soon."

"Does my brother know?"

Maeve shook her head. "Not yet. It will take hours I am afraid. There is no need to upset him now."

Brianna thought there was every reason to inform her brother. "I came up because you were not at breakfast."

Maeve managed a weak smile. "No food today. Not possible." She bent over and groaned. "The contractions are growing stronger. Perhaps you will do me the favor of sending for the midwife. No doubt she has been expecting this call."

Brianna took the information from Maeve and hurried downstairs. She found Ellis conversing with her brother in the breakfast room.

"Her Grace has begun her labor. Please inform Ralph and have him bring Mrs. Sedgewick here as soon as possible."

Her brother jumped up. "What? Is it that time already?" He turned to the butler. "Hurry, man!"

"I am certain Maeve will be fine," Brianna said trying her best to sound reassuring.

"I will go upstairs and be with her," the duke said. "I still want to call for the doctor. Maeve has stubbornly refused, claiming she trusts the midwife more, but I am not as certain." He did appear anxious.

Brianna followed her brother upstairs, although she could not keep pace with his long strides. He burst into Maeve's private quarters.

"My darling, why did you not inform me earlier?" He took his wife into his arms and kissed her passionately.

Maeve moaned and he released her. "The contractions began slowly during the night. I thought to wait until morning before telling you. There was really nothing you could have done for me."

"I could send for Dr. Raymond. He is an experienced accoucheur."

Maeve shook her head. "No, as I told you before, I prefer Mrs. Sedgewick. She has delivered over a hundred babies. She is knowledgeable. Trust me. It will be fine."

The duke turned to Brianna. "Go downstairs and make certain Ralph is on his way to get that midwife."

She nodded and left her brother holding his wife in his arms.

IT WAS OVER an hour before the midwife arrived. The duke was beside himself worrying for Maeve, although she kept reassuring him. Brianna did her best as well. It was a relief when Mrs. Sedgewick arrived and immediately took charge.

"You, sir, must go," she said to the duke.

When he protested, she gave him a hard look. "No men here. You are a nuisance. You get in the way of what needs to be done." The woman with graying hair was hefty with strong wrists and hands. It was obvious that she was not easily impressed or intimidated by anyone including aristocrats.

"Best leave us, for now," Maeve told him.

"You can stay," the midwife said to Brianna. "First, I want you to send me several maids. I will give them instructions on what is needed. I see the laying-in cot is already set up," she said approvingly.

Brianna left the room on the heels of her brother. She found Gwen and her sister-in-law's maid nearby, both waiting and expecting to help. The household was apparently on alert. Brianna decided to stay with her brother. He sent word to Lord Randall who came quickly to keep him company as well. The duke paced the drawing room for hours.

"Old man, you are going to wear out that fine Aubusson carpet at the rate you are going," Lord Randall said.

"Carpet be hanged!"

There was no dinner that evening, just a cold collation. No one had any appetite anyway. Finally, at eleven, Gwen came running down the stairs.

"Your Grace, your daughter has arrived. The midwife is sending for you."

They all hurried up the stairs, eager to meet the new arrival. Maeve looked exhausted but she was smiling and holding her new baby in her arms.

"Come see our child," she urged.

The midwife gently took the baby from her mother and placed her into her father's arms.

"Hold her so," the midwife cautioned. "Her head must be supported."

The swaddled baby whimpered but did not cry. Brianna saw the little red face.

"Is she not beautiful? Just like her mother," the duke said. "We must get the wet nurse here immediately."

"No," Maeve said. "This is something I wish to do myself. I will nurse my own child."

"Must you be so difficult?" He sighed deeply.

"You know very well you were intrigued because the ton considered me an original."

"Of course, you banished the ennui from my existence and brought me joy in its place."

"It is the way of the Romany," Maeve acknowledged. "I will raise our daughter in its ways as well as yours."

Brianna half-expected her brother to argue the point, saying this was not done by ladies of the aristocracy. However, he did not. Maeve made her own rules as everyone knew. One did not argue with her when her mind was made up, not even the Duke of Clarmont.

THE NEXT SEVERAL weeks passed swiftly. Maeve and her brother decided on names they both liked. Their daughter would be Margaret Alexandra—Margaret for Maeve's mother Magdelana and Alexandra for the last Duke of Clarmont,

Alexander, Adam's father. Their daughter was thriving, and the proud parents could not have been more pleased.

Brianna spent a good deal of time with Maeve and Margaret, but she was feeling dejected. She did not hear from James. His mother sent a beautiful gown for the baby, but there was no visit. It seemed they had cut off contact. It was disheartening. Yet what could she expect? James, it seemed, had no desire to court her, to pay his addresses. She did her best not to feel despondent, but it was not easy. Maeve understood her feelings without needing any explanation.

Would she ever see James again, she wondered. *What were his feelings toward her?*

CHAPTER FORTY-ONE

OCTOBER BEGAN THE SEASON OFFICIALLY. The Royal Family was back in residence and the aristocracy flocked back to London. The Duchess of Pemworth did as she had promised, and Brianna received the vouchers to Almack's that were significant to a debutante's success.

Almack's ballroom had glittering gilded columns, silk draperies, and rows of chandeliers. She soon discovered it also had sour lemonade and dry cakes. The duke had explained to her that the Patronesses of Almack's were the arbiters of London society and respectability. Their approval was necessary.

The Duchess of Pemworth took Brianna aside to a quiet corner to subtly point out each of the ladies. "That one is Lady Jersey. She can be rude, but you must always show her deference. She introduced the quadrille here last year. Lady Melbourne as you can see is quite attractive. She is also popular and wields a great deal of influence."

Brianna nodded her understanding, and the Duchess resumed her tutorial.

"Countess Lieven is a foreigner." The Duchess sniffed her disapproval. "She is married to the Russian ambassador. A bit haughty for my tastes. Mrs. Drummond-Burrell on the other hand is a Scot and Scottish reels are named for her. She is a stickler for the rules of propriety, but not as much so as Lady Castlereagh, wife of the Foreign Minister, who closes the doors at eleven p.m. and once refused entry to Wellington for coming later. Lady Sefton is the oldest of the group. Princess

Esterhazy is married to the Austrian Ambassador. You will find she demands attention."

"They are attractive ladies," Brianna observed.

"I daresay most of them are not much older than you, my dear. I will bring you around to converse with them. Bob a polite curtsy naturally and lower your eyes in deference."

"Thank you for your kindness," Brianna said. Her heart was not in this, but she did her best to fit into the illustrious society.

In speaking to some of the other girls, Brianna discovered that she was one of the older young ladies, most being seventeen or eighteen years in age. Several giggled when gentlemen approached and asked them to dance. Lord Randall had come and engaged her in a quadrille. Brianna was certain it was to oblige her brother.

Simon Andrews also engaged her in a vigorous country dance. He stood with her for a while. "Dreadfully boring these affairs," he whispered to her.

"If you find them so dull, why are you here?" she asked, arching a brow.

He pointed to a young girl sipping lemonade. "My cousin. I promised to be here for her. But I am not sorry I came. I did want to see you again." His manner was flirtatious, and it made her smile.

Lord Randall approached. "I say there, Andrews, do not monopolize the loveliest demoiselle here."

"Did not think you noticed anything but horseflesh. Been to any interesting races lately?" The tone was clearly sarcastic.

Brianna felt the tension building between the two men and thought to diffuse it. "Frightfully warm. I would really like something to drink," she said to Lord Randall and then fanned herself for emphasis.

"I will be right back," Lord Randall said.

She turned to Simon Andrews. "I enjoyed our dance. Thank you." She spoke dismissively and then quickly walked away to join the Duchess of Pemworth who took her by the arm.

"You are a success," the duchess said, her chins bobbing. "We have done well."

Brianna was not certain that she cared.

PRESENTATION TO THE Queen was another established formality. The Duchess of Pemworth was her sponsor here as well. It was explained to Brianna that not everyone was so honored. However, Brianna did not consider it much of an honor. For one thing, a special gown had to be made in the style of the Georgian era with a hoop skirt and feathers. It was heavy and uncomfortable, even with the high waist of the current style. Brianna thought she looked ridiculous in it.

She sat outside the South Queen's Drawing Room with other young ladies who were also to be presented in their uncomfortable gowns. The wait seemed to take forever. When she finally was called for her turn to be greeted by Queen Charlotte, Brianna rose stiffly. She entered the drawing room with its blue wallpaper and waited with her head bowed. When her name was called, Brianna came forward and knelt before the queen. Although already up in years, the queen had an amiable smile. She leaned over and kissed Brianna on the forehead. Brianna understood that this was a particular honor. The queen typically only offered her hand to be kissed and nothing more.

Brianna stood and backed away, doing her best not to stumble over the train of her skirt. She had been given instructions not to look behind her, nor was she allowed to turn her back on the queen. By the time she arrived back at Clarmont House, Brianna was exhausted. It had been a stressful experience.

CHAPTER FORTY-TWO

MAEVE HAD JUST FINISHED NURSING the baby. The nanny they hired took Margaret for a diaper change and nap.

Brianna told Maeve all about her debut at Almack's and her visit to Court. They sat down together upstairs in Maeve's private sitting room adjacent to her bed chamber. Brianna knew that Maeve's bed was rarely used at night because she and the duke preferred to sleep together in his chamber. Gwen had shared that bit of information with her some time ago. The servants always knew things and enjoyed gossiping.

"Your presentation at court sounds exciting," Maeve said. "Did you enjoy yourself?"

Brianna shook her head. "Not really, but for my brother's sake, I did what was expected of me."

"What did you think of Queen Charlotte?"

"She is quite impressive. She was also kind to me."

"You are the daughter and sister of a peer of the realm. It is to be expected."

"Will you be presented at court as you are the wife of a peer of the realm?"

Maeve gave a dubious shrug. "I suppose Adam would arrange it if I truly wanted that distinction, but I do not. I am perfectly satisfied not to indulge overly in the social whirl of the aristocracy. Adam understands that and accepts it. Your situation is different. You are now officially on the marriage mart."

Brianna groaned.

Maeve took her hand, eyes owl gray and luminous. "It is not a bad thing. You will meet many gentlemen. You will form friendships with other young women your age. Eventually, you will find a husband that suits you. There was a time when I only wanted my freedom, to join the Romany. I soon learned it was not enough. The best part of living is to find someone who loves you and you can love in return. You will see."

Brianna had an opportunity to become part of the ton for the first time several evenings later. There was to be a ball in honor of her coming out into society. The staff was busy from morning until night getting the ballroom ready for the company. It had not been used in years and needed considerable attention.

Brianna and Maeve had been fitted for elegant new gowns. They stood with her brother on the receiving line as an impressive group of people was announced. Brianna did not believe she would ever remember all their names. It made her head swim.

Candles lit the crystal chandeliers. The ceiling had been repainted vividly with angels, cherubs, harps and trumpets now hovering in an azure sky. There were gilded pillars and pots of fragrant flowers everywhere on the perimeters of the large room. Piles of fruit and delectable dainties were piled high on platters on long tables covered with fine white linen tablecloths. There were also drinks to refresh the guests before supper was served. Wall mirrors were polished and glistened. The orchestra was on the dais. The dance floor gleamed with fresh polish as well. And all of this was in her honor. Brianna could not help but be impressed.

In the first dance of the evening, she was led out to the floor by her brother. They lined up for a Pavilion Quadrille. Lord Randall requested the second dance with Brianna which was less lively. It was a minuet that the duke led out with his wife. Later there were country dances and reels with different partners which left her breathless. Eventually, she joined Maeve and the Duchess of Pemworth who wore a large turquoise turban with peacock feathers on her head.

"I am out of breath," Brianna said, fanning herself vigorously.

Maeve laughed. "I am not at all surprised."

Brianna looked around the room.

"Some parti you are especially looking for?" the Duchess of Pemworth asked.

"Mr. Winthrop and Mrs. Anna Winthrop were invited as I had instructed, were they not?"

"Yes, dear, in fact, I believe they have just arrived." Maeve nodded in a direction close to the entrance to the ballroom. "Welcome them by all means."

Brianna sought them out eagerly. "So glad you could come."

Anna Winthrop took her hands in her own. "My dear, you look so beautiful tonight. Does she not, James."

He nodded. "Sparkling like a star in the sky."

She thought he was probably referring to the shimmering white silk of her gown sewn discreetly with bead pearls in the modest bodice. Still, it was a flattering comment.

"I am sorry we are so late to arrive, but James was held up at work."

"Oh, that is no problem," Brianna said.

"I will not invite you to dance with me," James said. "I have the dance steps of an elephant and would only crush your poor feet in those satin slippers."

There was excitement in the crowd, and Brianna wondered about it. Voices were raised. The Duchess of Pemworth hurried across the ballroom to Brianna.

"Word has just arrived. We are to be honored by an appearance of the Prince Regent."

Her brother joined them. "Come, we must welcome him. He is to arrive at any moment."

Known as Prinny, the Prince Regent, did come briefly. They bowed and curtsied deeply to him. Brianna's impression was of a man of considerable girth. He demanded that the French doors be closed, although it was warm in the room with so many people present. He removed a snuff box, took a whiff, and promptly sneezed. Then he joined the Duchess of Pemworth and flirted with her placing his hand on her backside which Brianna found surprising. Brianna thought the royal prince fat and self-indulgent. Her brother introduced the Prince to Maeve and Brianna. He was polite but clearly disinterested. He did not remain long.

As soon as the prince left, the French doors were opened again to allow in the air. Her brother was in high spirits. The social event was now considered a great success.

However, Brianna was not as sanguine as her brother. When she again looked for James and Anna, she found that they had left. She had hoped to sit with them for supper.

Instead, Lord Randall engaged her for the supper dance which meant he would be her companion. Although the food served was of the very best, she found herself having little appetite for it.

"Do have some of this white soup," Lord Randall said.

She shook her head. Undaunted, Howard collected sundry dainties to tempt her. She ended up nibbling on a lobster pate and sliced ham just to please him, washing it down with Champagne.

~♥~

BRIANNA SLEPT IN the following day. They had been up until three in the morning. She was told that was considered early by ton standards.

Maeve was yawning when Brianna sought her out. "You look tired," Maeve said.

"I am. You must be exhausted too."

Maeve shook her head. "I left after dinner was served. It was late but I was done in by then. Of course, you could not leave your own ball. Did you have a wonderful time?"

Brianna flopped down on Maeve's bed. "To a point."

"You were upset that Mr. Winthrop and his mother did not stay longer?"

Brianna stared at her sister-in-law. "It amazes me how perceptive you are."

Maeve offered a modest shrug. "Simply a matter of observation. He watched you dance for a time. He looked at you longingly. I do believe he cares deeply for you."

"Why does he not act then? It is so frustrating."

"Something does hold him back as I previously observed. If I could give him a reading, I might be able to find out what it is. Let us talk about the ball instead. What did you think of Prinny?"

"I was surprised that he flirted with the Duchess of Pemworth."

"I was not," Maeve said.

Brianna gave her a questioning look.

"He loves to flirt with older women. It is one of his idiosyncrasies."

"Not younger women?"

Maeve shook her head. "It is well-known."

Brianna pondered human nature. Perhaps she would never understand people—James Winthrop in particular. She let out a deep sigh.

CHAPTER FORTY-THREE

JAMES THOUGHT ABOUT BRIANNA CONSTANTLY. He was out of sorts, angry with himself. Why could he not forget about her? She was out of his life, in an entirely different sphere.

His mother sat down beside him on the settee in their drawing room. "Tired after last night?" she asked.

He shook his head.

"Problems at work? I know you were set back by all the ugliness in court."

"No, the business is doing well. Even when I am not present, it runs smoothly, thanks to the acumen of Father. He hired trustworthy people. He also left us well-fixed financially in all respects."

"Then what is troubling you? I know there is something."

James leaned forward, placing his face in his hands. "It is nothing. It will pass."

"Ah, I see. It is Brianna. You regretted attending her ball however briefly."

"Best to forget her. She was with us only a short time."

His mother placed her hand on his. "But you cannot forget her, can you? And why should you?"

James sat up and faced his mother squarely. "We are from two very different worlds."

"That would not matter to her."

"Even if that were the case, do you not understand that it is impossible for me to consider a life with her."

His mother stood up. "No, I do not see that at all. You looked at her with admiration yesterday evening and I saw the looks she sent to you as well. She was not interested in any of the young bucks that presented themselves to her, only you."

"I cannot listen to this foolish, romantic rot."

"And I do not understand your foolish behavior. It infuriates me."

James looked up. He could not remember the last time his mother had expressed such anger toward him. His temper flared as well.

"Am I to understand you? You wish me to court a woman, knowing that if I did marry her, the relationship could only end in disaster?"

"Whatever are you talking about?" His mother appeared bewildered.

James got to his feet and faced her. "When Father was dying, his doctor explained to me that he had a rare illness, one that eventually paralyzed him completely. He also told me that it was genetic, passed down from one generation to the next. I recalled then that no one in Father's family lived a long life. Is this not why you chose to have no more than one child?"

His mother met his searching gazing with directness. "There are things you do not know about, things I should have told you long ago, but I was too proud, too ashamed. Your father urged me to do so, but in the end, he accepted that it was my decision to make. Now I realize that I have done you a grave injustice."

They were interrupted by the housekeeper who insisted that there was some matter in the kitchen that needed his mother's immediate attention. James was left hanging. What possible thing could his mother need to tell him that would make a difference in his relationship with Brianna? Likely, she was just trying to matchmake because she was so fond of Brianna and wanted the girl back in their home. Yet he found himself waiting impatiently for his mother's return. He began pacing the room. Finally, his mother returned and closed the drawing room doors. She resumed her seat beside him.

"What I have to say I have shared with no one else except your father." She took a deep breath and slowly let it out. "I was once young and foolish. My father was a baronet. Our family lived in the country. We were comfortable. I had three sisters. I was the eldest. My father intended that one day I would marry the oldest son of our local squire. He was prosperous and his oldest son was his heir.

"There was but one problem. I loved his third son, and he loved me. When the squire learned of this, he said it was time for Samuel to go out into the world. He purchased a commission for my sweetheart. The squire believed his second son was to become a clergyman while Samuel should be an army officer." His mother fidgeted in her chair. She looked off into space as if reliving that time in her life.

"Samuel was as broken-hearted as I was, but he swore that he would come home, and we would be married when he was on leave. We made love the night before he left. He did not force me. I gave my virginity freely. Then I waited and waited for his return. But that never happened. The family received word that he was killed on foreign soil. I never knew the exact details. By then, I was feeling sick, nauseated every morning. My family thought I had some illness—until I began increasing. My mother realized it first. I was with child. My parents were appalled. How could that be, they asked. I told them the truth.

"At first, my father intended to beat me. My mother stayed his hand. But then he decided something much worse. I was to be banished from the family. My name was never to be spoken of again. 'Get out and never come back', my father said. He told me I was no longer his daughter. My mother wept. I never even got to say goodbye to my younger sisters. I never saw any of them again. I traveled by mail coach to London, an arduous trip. Once here, like Brianna, I was confused. I had very little money. I thought of finding myself some employment, but in the obvious condition I was in, no one would consider hiring me for any kind of work. Although I located the least expensive lodging, my reserve of coin soon ran out. I could not be a beggar or worse. I could not live on the streets in a strange city where I knew no one. I soon decided I must end my life."

"Oh, Mother, no!" He took her cold hand, but she turned away from him. He saw that tears were running down her cheeks. Her story horrified him.

His mother choked back her tears, vigorously rubbing them from her face. "I must continue," she said. "You have a right to know everything." He saw there was a tremor in her hands. He wanted her to stop this painful confession, yet at the same time, he needed to hear it.

"I decided to jump from a bridge and drown in the water."

James let out a gasp.

"I started to climb up, but strong hands grabbed me and brought me down. 'You must not do this,' the man said. I collapsed in his arms, and he held me close." His mother turned and looked him in the eye. "James, that man was your father."

He was confused. "My father?"

"He was your father in every respect except conceiving you. Your father had no intention of marrying because of his illness. He planned to let his line die out. He planned to leave a will donating a considerable amount of the vast family fortune to various charities. However, he changed his life for me. He took me home with him and treated me with the utmost respect and kindness. He married me. How could I not love such a fine man? He gave me everything and he raised you as his own child. You were his son in every way that mattered. But you are not of his blood. If the thought of transmitting his illness to your offspring is what stops you from considering marriage, you should know that impediment does not exist."

"You are right. You should have told me this a long time ago." His mind was reeling from her confession.

His mother turned away again. "I could not bring myself to do it. I did not want you to think less of me. But seeing you suffer this way caused me to realize that it was necessary. I was being selfish."

Suddenly, a lot of things that had puzzled him regarding his mother made sense. She had never spoken of her family, never mentioned being disinherited by her father. She had been treated cruelly to his mind. She had been relatively reclusive, reserved and withdrawn all his life. Only with his father and himself had she shown love and vitality.

And now he understood why his mother had been so sympathetic to Brianna and her plight. He had wondered why she insisted on bringing the girl home with them and offering a position in their household. His mother obviously had seen in Brianna a girl like herself, cast off and struggling to exist.

"May I ask what your feelings are for Brianna?" his mother asked. She had regained some measure of composure.

"My head spins at the moment with all you have told me."

"She is a special young woman. She would make you a fine wife."

"But would I be the right husband for her? When she was here in this house, perhaps things were different. You saw her at her ball. She was in her element. She fits in with those people. I do not."

"You are as good as any of them—better really. You create employment for many people. You are an important person in keeping England a world power. So many lives are benefited by what you do each day."

He kissed his mother on the cheek, smiling. "Spoken like a loving mother."

"It is all true. I hope you do not think less of me for what I have told you."

He looked at her and thought at this moment, she looked older than her years. He realized how difficult this talk had been for her. "I will always love you dearly. Be assured of that."

She looked relieved.

"You have given me a great deal to think about."

CHAPTER FORTY-FOUR

After her ball, Brianna received many invitations. The Season was in full swing. Over breakfast, she examined some of the offers. Her brother joined her, helping himself to the dishes on the sideboard. They enjoyed a hearty meal of ham, grilled kidneys, buttered eggs, muffins and strong coffee.

"I see you are enjoying some popularity," the duke observed.

"It is somewhat bewildering, to say the least. Look at all of this. Balls, soirees, Venetian breakfasts, picnics, evenings at Vauxhall Gardens, masquerades. There are also theatre invitations for the new plays as well as for the opera." She shook her head. "It is too much."

"Fustian. You should feel flattered. So many ladies and gentlemen wish to further their acquaintance with you."

She rose, fluffing out the soft yellow muslin dress with its flounce. "I cannot look at all of this right now."

Her brother shook his head. "You can expect callers this afternoon."

"All those flowers cause me to sneeze."

The duke laughed. She left him, thinking to herself how much she wished one of those callers would be James Winthrop.

~♥~

BRIANNA SPENT MOST of the morning examining the invitations she had received and writing a few responses. For the most part, she did not know the individuals who sent the invitations and once she had removed those she would not accept out of hand, she decided to discuss the others with Maeve and the duke. They would better know which ones were unexceptionable and which were not. She did not wish to make a faux pau which might embarrass her brother. But there was one invitation she immediately decided to accept, and which made her happy.

Brianna found Maeve in the nursery playing with her baby daughter. "Margaret looks so happy and content," Brianna observed.

Maeve smiled. "She is. Maggie has been steadily gaining weight and growing. It is a delight to be with her."

Brianna thought of her own mother. She doubted Mama had ever felt that way, at least not about her. "You are a very good mother," she said.

Maeve smiled at the compliment. "Did you wish to discuss something with me?"

As usual, Maeve was perceptive.

"I do. I received a number of invitations and would like to have you examine some of them with me. You know the ton far better than I do."

Maeve kissed her baby's forehead. "Actually, I do not. We shall consult Adam. He will know. I believe he will be out all day. However, we can discuss it after dinner this evening."

"There is one invitation that I will accept immediately."

Maeve quirked an eyebrow.

"It is from Anna Winthrop. She has invited me to afternoon tea tomorrow."

"And you wish to go."

Brianna nodded. "I do."

"May I ask one favor?"

"Of course," Brianna quickly said.

"Fleur is not happy here. She is restless. Perhaps you will take her with you tomorrow. Her testimony did save James Winthrop's life after all. I believe she would be welcome."

"A splendid idea," Brianna agreed.

"I will have Ralph go with you. He will ride next to our coachman."

"Must we trouble him?" Brianna asked.

"Mr. Brockton would be displeased if he thought Ralph was not guarding your safety."

"Very well," Brianna said, although she believed Maeve was being overly protective.

BRIANNA WAS ALL nerves the following day. All she could think about was going back to the Winthrop's home. Would James be there? Unlikely, of course, he had a huge business to run. Still, if Anna asked him to come to tea, Brianna knew he would accommodate his parent. He was a considerate and loving son.

Fleur fussed about coming on the visit with her. "I don't know those people, Miss, and they won't want to know me for certain."

"But you testified for James. You saved his life. You have earned their gratitude. They will welcome you. Please visit with me. I would feel better."

Fleur pursed her lips. "Well, only as a favor to you. But I don't have nothing polite-like to wear."

"You may again select something from my closet for now. We talked about shopping. You deserve a new wardrobe. We will visit the modiste in a day or two."

Suddenly Fleur was smiling. She looked much younger and prettier with all the heavy make-up removed. Fleur selected a green muslin that Brianna had yet to wear. However, she was more than happy to give it to Fleur.

When they went out to the waiting carriage, Ralph was there to greet them. His homely face lit up at the sight of Fleur. "Ladies," he said, "you are both in looks. A pleasure to serve you."

Fleur, in turn, smiled at him. "Help me into the carriage," she said in a husky, flirtatious voice.

Brianna wondered about it. Was something developing between Fleur and Ralph?

Just as she would have expected, Anna Winthrop greeted them warmly. "I am so happy that you have come today. Both of you are most welcome. I hope you do not mind a bit of male company as well. I asked James to join us."

Brianna's heart began to beat more rapidly. She was eager to see him, but how would he feel about her? As it turned out, she did not have long to wait.

Tea was served in the drawing room. Anna was a warm and amiable hostess. She put both Fleur and her at ease. Fleur had already stuffed down two raspberry pastries by the time James joined them. He kissed his mother's cheek, sat down on a straight-back chair, and acknowledged both Fleur and her. He looked incredibly handsome. Brianna realized she had been holding her breath and let it out slowly.

"It is good to see you," James said to Brianna.

"I feel the same," she said, not quite meeting his eyes.

Anna must have felt the tension between James and her because she kept up a steady stream of conversation, mostly with Fleur.

"Do you like being a guest at Clarmont House?" Anna asked Fleur.

"It's all right I guess." Fleur shrugged indifferently.

"But life must be better for you," Anna said, putting down her teacup.

Fleur folded her hands together. "I appreciates all they done for me. But I'm not one to sit still. I mean, there's not much for me to do there. It ain't comfortable-like. Seems like rich ladies lead boring lives."

Anna was thoughtful. "Do you like to read? There must be a library in the house or a lending library to which to subscribe."

Fleur shook her head. "That ain't for me. I can barely read a word. I don't like painting pictures like Miss Brianna does and I don't play no instruments either."

Anna turned her head to one side. "I understand you are a practical person. I enjoy doing needlepoint. It relaxes me. Why not come with me, and I will show you some of my work. Perhaps that or crocheting might interest you."

"All right," Fleur agreed with some hesitation and reluctance.

Anna led her out of the room, closing the drawing room doors behind them. Brianna observed that she was smiling. James immediately put his teacup down and turned to face her.

"Mother thought to give us some time alone."

Brianna offered a conceding nod. "Yes, that is obvious to me as well."

"Are you enjoying your come out into society?" His gaze was fixed on hers.

"To an extent. You left my ball early."

"Mother and I felt out of place there. We knew few people."

"You knew me," she said.

"You were the center of attention. We came and paid our respects."

"James, I am not a snob."

He looked hurt. "I never thought you were."

"Truth be told, I knew very few of those people either."

James lowered his gaze. "You will become one of them eventually."

She stood up and came close to him. "I am not certain of that. Maeve says telling a man you have feelings for him is not appropriate. But I do have feelings for you, James. Do you feel the same way about me? If you do not, then I accept it, but I feel I must speak."

JAMES WAS OVERWHELMED by emotion. He never would have expected Brianna to make such a declaration. He suddenly realized that he was free to ask a woman to marry him if he so chose. His mother's confession changed everything. But could a match between an aristocrat and a bourgeois be a happy one? Was he being a snob in reverse? These were questions without answers. No one could know what the future would bring. Marriage was a gamble at best. What he did know was that he loved Brianna. He had fought those feelings, but he did not want to continue to do so.

James took Brianna in his arms and kissed her. At first, the kiss was gentle, a mere meeting of lips. But then stronger emotions took over. He felt a hunger in his heart and soul, a need, a desire. She must have felt the same because she kissed him back passionately. His tongue caressed and licked her lips with liquid fire. Finally, it plunged provocatively inside. With one hand he reached up to caress and then cup her breast. His hand unbuttoned her bodice as he trailed kisses down to the exposed swell of tender flesh.

BRIANNA MOANED, FEELING his heat and hunger. Her breasts were crushed against the hard wall of his chest. This intimacy was what she wanted and needed, what she craved. Yet for the sake of decency, she realized they could go no further. She moved away from him and fixed her bodice. He gave her a speaking look. He seemed as breathless as she was.

"I will make my addresses to your brother and let my intentions be known if you choose to marry me."

"Yes, I would like that above all else."

He took her into his arms and kissed her again. Then they sat down side by side on the settee. He kissed the palm of each of her hands. She felt a tingling sensation.

"Shall we tell your mother?"

James shook his head. "Not until I have spoken to your brother."

"I will talk with him as well," she said.

"I am glad you came today," he told her.

"Of course, your mother's invitation was the first to which I responded."

He offered a wry smile. "I was a bit surprised you brought Fleur with you."

"Why is that?"

"Well, to put it delicately, she is hardly the kind of person I would expect you to associate with."

Brianna frowned. "Maeve suggested I invite her to accompany me. Fleur is responsible for saving you from a noose."

"I apologize. I meant no disrespect. However, you are so pure and innocent while she is..." he broke off.

Brianna felt her cheeks flush. She rose to her feet. "I must leave."

James looked alarmed. "Have I offended you? I do apologize for speaking so bluntly."

She shook her head. "No, I must go now."

She hurried from the drawing room. Fortunately, she met Anna and Fleur in the hallway.

"Fleur, I must leave now."

"Oh, must you?" Anna said looking disappointed.

"Yes, I am afraid so."

Fleur nodded her assent. Anna sent a maid to retrieve their pelisses. Ralph was waiting nearby with the carriage. Fleur said nothing until they were settled inside. Finally, she turned to Brianna.

"What's the matter?"

Brianna shook her head. She could not manage to speak. She had been carried away by desire and had not used her head. She needed time alone to think.

CHAPTER FORTY-FIVE

BRIANNA WENT STRAIGHT TO HER bedroom, not wishing to see or talk to anyone. She was angry. How could he say that to her? How could he ruin everything in that way! She was furious. She paced her room striding back and forth.

There was a knock and Gwen entered. She cast a doubtful look in Brianna's direction. "Fleur said you were in a taking, Miss. If you aren't feeling well, Cook can mix you a dose of hartshorn and water. Make you feel more the thing."

"That will not fix my problem, Gwen. But thank you for the thought."

"Can I get you anything at all?" Worry lines appeared on Gwen's forehead.

"No, you can go. I need to be alone for now." Gwen left her, still with a look of concern.

Brianna had considered James a man of breeding and common sense. Now she had to wonder. Were all men like him? Perhaps they were. She would discuss this with Maeve, as she did so many things. Her sister-in-law usually had good insights. All she knew now was that as matters stood, she would have to refuse the proposal, and that would surely break her heart.

Brianna did not go down for dinner. A tray was brought up to her. She barely touched it. That night, she slept poorly. There were bad dreams. A horrible dream woke her in the middle of the night, and she could not return to sleep. She realized what James said about Fleur caused her to recall an experience she had long ago done her best to forget. But it did happen, and the comment James made caused her to be reminded and relive it in her nightmare. Yes, she must talk with Maeve. There was no other way to deal with this, she realized.

IN THE MORNING, the baby was fussing, and Maeve stayed in the nursery until Maggie took her nap at noon. Brianna had lunch with her.

"You look tired," Brianna said.

"You as well," Maeve observed.

"I suppose we both have our reasons. I believe I need to discuss a matter of some urgency with you, if you are not too worn out."

Maeve smiled. "I always have time for you. We are sisters."

They finished their light meal and Brianna followed Maeve to her private quarters.

"I am assuming you wish to talk without anyone else listening," Maeve said.

"You are quite right. Where do I begin?"

"Take a seat," Maeve said. She made certain the door was closed.

Brianna appreciated that Maeve could always be counted upon to be discreet. She took the comfortable chair near the bed, an elegant piece with gold claw feet, while Maeve seated herself on her ornate dressing chair which matched.

"Now you must explain what has you so upset."

Brianna let out a deep sigh. "James asked me to marry him yesterday."

"How wonderful! Did you accept?" Maeve's intense eyes were bright with interest.

"At first, yes, I did accept. But I now realize it would be impossible for me to marry him."

"I do not understand." Maeve shook her head in bewilderment.

"James made a comment about Fleur. I believe he thought it inappropriate that a pure and innocent person such as myself should associate with her kind." Brianna paused.

"Continue please," Maeve urged.

"I am neither pure nor innocent." Brianna lowered her gaze. Her cheeks flushed with shame.

"I do not believe that. You are talking such moonshine," Maeve said.

Brianna shook her head. "No, it is the truth. Where to begin?"

"At the beginning, of course," Maeve said.

"It began with my mother. Mama was no better than she ought to be. Mama had lovers. Throughout my childhood, we traveled extensively. She was a restless soul, never long happy with one place or one man. I saw little of her in fact. In Italy, for a time, she was the mistress of a very wealthy count. He showered her with gifts. But he was a man devoid of a moral compass." She took a deep breath and let it out slowly. How could she tell anyone, even Maeve? But she must.

"I was eleven when the incident occurred. I was asleep in bed when I was awakened by someone's hands groping me. I started to cry out, but he would not stop. He put his hand over my mouth. He said, 'My child, it is me, coming to give you the love you deserve.' I bit his hand. I was terrified. Even at that age, I knew he was not supposed to touch me intimately. He hit me then and I fought him. He pushed his member into me, and I screamed. The pain was terrible. Our maid was woken by the noise and came running. When Mama heard of what happened, she insisted that the count leave the house and not come back. I was bleeding and crying. I thought Mama would comfort me, but she did the opposite. She was furious with me. She blamed me. She said I had enticed him. I was shocked. I hardly knew him. But Mama insisted that it had been my fault. Soon we were on our way to Switzerland. Her mission was to enroll me in school and leave me there. That was the best thing that ever happened to me in my life."

Maeve took Brianna in her arms and hugged her. "Your mother was wrong and unfair. None of what happened was your fault."

Brianna pulled away. "But you see now why I say I am not pure or innocent. Maeve, I am not a virgin. If I married James, clearly that is what he would expect. If I told him the sordid details of my past, what would he think of me? It is insupportable."

"My dear, if he truly loves you, as I believe he does, he will be sympathetic and understanding. He will not think less of you."

"Do you really think so?"

"Yes, I do."

Tears streamed down Brianna's cheeks. She had not been aware that she was crying. The emotions of recalling and recounting the horrible incident she had long ago repressed and buried in the past had overwhelmed her.

"I consider it quite unfair that men may do as they like. They are often admired for having relations with many women, whereas if a woman seeks the same freedom she is dubbed a whore. Perhaps attitudes will change with time, but it is still an injustice." Maeve frowned.

"Maeve, what should I do?"

"You should trust James. If he is the man you think him to be, he will listen and accept what you tell him. I believe he does love you. Be honest with him. It is the only way to start a relationship. You are right not to accept his proposal until that is done."

Brianna nodded. Of course, Maeve was right. She saw that clearly now. "I will talk with him as soon as possible."

She left Maeve, lost in thought. Walking down the hall corridor, she thought of Fleur. They had visited the Winthrops together and Brianna had the distinct impression that Fleur was not comfortable or happy living in the ducal mansion. Perhaps she would do well thinking of helping Fleur rather than just considering her own problems. She did not wish to be selfish and inconsiderate of others.

Brianna stopped outside of Fleur's room. She was about to knock when she heard odd noises coming from inside. There were moans and groans somewhat muffled. Was Fleur ill? Did she need help? Brianna hurriedly opened the unlocked door and rushed in.

"Fleur, what is wrong? Do you need help?"

Brianna had the shock of her life. There in bed stark naked lay Fleur on top of Ralph. There was no misinterpreting what they were doing. Brianna, red-faced with embarrassment, wished she could simply disappear.

Fleur moved off Ralph, gathering a sheet over her still-exposed body. "Miss, don't you think to knock?"

"I am sorry. I thought you were ill and in pain."

Fleur smiled, exposing yellowed teeth. "Girl, I was in the throes of pleasure."

"Sorry, I will go," Brianna said, moving quickly to the door.

"Wait," Ralph called to her. He was sitting up now, his hairy barrel chest in view. "I wants you to be the first to know that me and Fleur is going to get married, right and proper. We was just kind of celebrating in advance."

"That is wonderful. Fleur, we will shop for a trousseau in the next few days. You must tell Maeve and the duke so that they will have a proper wedding reception for you." With that, Brianna hurriedly left Fleur's room and firmly shut the door behind her.

She sought out Maeve again and told her what had happened. Maeve merely laughed.

"I do not find it amusing. I was mortified."

"You should have knocked. Of course, Fleur should have locked her door. However, since she and Ralph were in the throes of passion, we must excuse them."

"I told Fleur I would shop with her in the coming days. I have been promising to do so. Now it becomes imperative."

Maeve appeared thoughtful. "We did not know what to do about Fleur. It would seem she has solved that problem for herself."

Brianna agreed. If only her own problem could be solved as easily.

CHAPTER FORTY-SIX

A swirling gray mist surrounded their carriage as Brianna and Fleur headed to the shopping district. Fleur was in high spirits.

"Imagine me of all people shopping like a real lady! Why I can hardly believe it."

"You deserve it," Brianna assured her.

Ralph and their coachman let them out in front of the modiste's shop Brianna was familiar with. They waited outside while she and Fleur entered the shop. However, all the workers were busy. The shop was crowded. Fleur quickly became impatient.

"Let's look about. It's too la-di-da here anyway."

Fleur told Ralph that they were going to have a look at some other shops, and they agreed the carriage would wait there for them. They walked the length of Pall Mall. Brianna was glad she wore her comfortable kid half-boots. Her skirts fluttered for a few moments then settled across her legs. There was a chill in the air, a harbinger of a wet autumn.

Fleur peered into the window of a hat shop. "Look at that one, will you?" She pointed.

"You should try it on," Brianna said.

Fleur wasted no time entering the shop. She immediately fell in love with the buff-colored chip straw bonnet. It had a band of pink rosebuds around the rim. "I must have it," she said.

Brianna paid the shopkeeper and they continued on their way. In another location, Fleur was able to find several ready-made afternoon dresses. She was measured by a seamstress and promised that alterations could be made quickly. One afternoon dress of sprigged muslin was a good fit. Brianna paid for it and Fleur decided to wear it immediately.

"This is so fine," Fleur said, her cheeks rosy with excitement.

They were walking back down the street to their carriage when someone called out to Fleur. They turned and were faced with of all people Madam Louise.

"Where have the likes of you been?" she said to Fleur. Her expression was angry and accusing.

"I got a different life now," Fleur countered. She raised her chin combatively.

"No, you don't. You owes me. I'm taking you back to work for me." She turned to Brianna. "This one too."

"Absolutely not," Brianna said, folding her arms over her chest. "We are going nowhere with you."

Louise pointed a blood-red painted fingernail at Brianna. "Don't think I don't know that you took Fleur away and got her to speak for that young fellow."

"But that was all I did. I swear," Fleur responded, nervously biting down on her lower lip.

Louise pulled twin pistols from her outing jacket, one from each side pocket. One was pointed at her and the other toward Fleur who gasped.

"Don't shoot us!" Fleur cried.

"I won't if you come with me and don't make no fuss. Otherwise, I'll have to kill you both."

Something clicked in Brianna's mind, something she realized she should have thought of before. Was it too late now? Dear Lord, she hoped not.

"Gabe, put these two in the carriage and keep your eyes peeled on them. They are slippery as eels. If they try to get away, gut them with your knife." Louise offered an ugly smile as if the thought of them dead pleased her no end.

Brianna's heart was pounding. There had to be something she could do, but at the moment, her mind was blank. Gabe was a big man, well-muscled and mean-looking. He shoved them both forward toward a waiting carriage.

Brianna looked around, hoping to see someone who might help them. She planned to start screaming. She felt that if they got into the carriage, they were doomed. She gave the man a hard shove, but he did not budge. She started to yell for help, but he hit her on the side of the head, and she fell. Dizzy, Brianna felt herself being lifted.

~♥~

JAMES DROPPED HIS mother at the lending library. He planned to treat her to Gunther's after she made her selections. His mother was not feeling quite the thing. She had obviously believed that when she arranged for Brianna and him to spend some time alone a proposal would occur. That was, of course, what had happened. However, he was completely confused by the outcome. At first, Brianna had been very receptive. She accepted him with the utmost ardor. He was overjoyed. Then she literally ran from him.

What had he said to make her change so in such a manner? How had he insulted her? He merely stated that she was so different from Fleur, that it surprised him she should associate with such a person. He had not told his mother about his proposal, Brianna's acceptance, and then her apparent rejection. Mother was already disappointed. Still, he felt guilty, which was why he had offered to take her out this afternoon.

He saw the mist had finally begun to clear. He decided to leave the carriage and take a walk up the street. He had no desire to borrow the latest books from the lending library. At this hour, there were only ladies inside the shop. No doubt his mother would enjoy perusing some of the books with the other women for a time before making her own selections.

As he walked, James heard a commotion of some sort. There were angry voices. Someone was making threats. The voice was of a woman of the lower classes. He thought he recognized it. He kept walking in the direction of the voice. He saw the madame from Foxworth's brothel waving pistols at two young women. He focused and realized in horror that the women being threatened were Brianna and Fleur.

A large man with a menacing manner hit Brianna and carried her into a waiting coach. Fleur was forced in by the madam. James ran after them, but the coach took off before he could reach it. He must do something! Stop them somehow. He began to run back down the street wanting to follow them in his own coach.

A man stopped him, placing a heavily muscled arm on his shoulder. "Here now, Mr. Winthrop, is it? Where be you going in such a hurry?"

James saw that it was Ralph. He had never been more grateful to see anyone in his life.

"That madam from Foxworth's abducted Brianna and Fleur just a moment ago. I tried to stop them, but I wasn't quick enough." He spoke in a breathless voice and hoped Ralph fully understood him.

"I was just going to check on the ladies. They was shopping hereabouts. I know where the whore took them. It's back to that brothel. I'll be going there."

"The woman is armed," James warned.

"I've got pistols in the carriage. You coming?"

"Yes." He told Ralph he would first let his mother know that she must go back home unaccompanied, but the coach and driver were parked just outside the lending library.

James hurried back and told his mother he had an errand to run, that she must return home without him. He did not explain further, not wishing to upset her more than was necessary. Meanwhile, Ralph was waiting for him. They got into the ducal coach together. Ralph gave the coachman the address which he seemed to know. James did not bother to ask any questions. He had, after all, been there himself as well, though not for the usual reasons. He doubted Ralph had either.

~♥~

BRIANNA ROSE TO full consciousness feeling pain on the side of her head. She moaned slightly.

"Oh, Miss, so grateful you're alive. I wasn't certain for a time there."

Brianna's eyes fluttered open. She tried to focus. "Fleur, where are we."

"In Mr. Foxworth's coach—except now it belongs to Madame Louise."

Fear seized her by the throat. She hardly had time to think before the carriage came to an abrupt stop and she was thrown forward. Strong hands lifted her out. Her head spun and she felt nauseous and dizzy.

"This one's lookin' poorly," the man carrying her said, his voice deep.

"She's the one took our Fleur from here and got her to talk for that young fellow who should have swung. Don't feel no kindness for her." Madame Louise's words chilled her.

"What do you intend to do with us?" Brianna said, doing her best to focus her gaze on the madam.

"Put you to work on your backs," the madam said matter-of-factly.

"People will be searching for us," Brianna countered.

The madam gave a nasty laugh. "I doubt that."

The front door opened and then Brianna was dropped unceremoniously on the marble floor as if she were a sack of vegetables.

"I see you brought them two back." Brianna focused on Nell who was wiping her nose on the sleeve of her dress.

"That's right and take better charge of this one than you did before. She's a slippery eel." Madame Louise pointed to Brianna. Then she turned to Fleur. "And you, what did you tell them Runners about me?"

Fleur shook her head. She looked pale and frightened. "I said nothing. I never told how you killed Mr. Foxworth while he lay unconscious on the ground. All I told was that the young man didn't kill Foxworth, that he were still alive when the fellow left the alley."

Louise slapped her across the face. "That were more than you should have said. You'll work extra hard now to make up for leaving here with that one." She pointed an accusing finger at Brianna.

Fleur helped Brianna get up from the floor and steadied her. "If you hurt us, the men won't want us."

"Ha! They won't care," Louise said. She spoke now to Nell. "Take 'em upstairs and lock them up for now." Then she turned to her henchman. "You can stand guard down here, just in case some unwanted fellows turn up."

When Brianna was slow to move, Nell gave her a hard shove. There was no point offering further resistance at this time, Brianna realized. Someone would come for them. Ralph must realize by now that something was very wrong. They would not just disappear. But would he know to look for them here?

RALPH DID NOT have the coachman drive them directly to the brothel. "We need to let His Greatness know what's happening. He'll get the Runners out there lickety-split."

James knew what Ralph said made sense, but he was worried about Brianna. He felt it was a matter of urgency that they reach her as soon as possible. Clearly, she was in danger, and he wanted to protect her.

It seemed to him that the drive to Clarmont House took forever. Ralph appeared to sense his frustration.

"Patience, sir, we will be there shortly."

The butler greeted them at the door.

"Is the duke in residence at this time?" James was in no mood to be polite or civil.

"Yes, sir, he is in his study working with his man of affairs."

"Please let him know we are here and need to speak with him immediately on a matter of utmost urgency."

The butler did not argue with him, instead left them where they stood. James was impatient. Every moment lost was another that placed Brianna in harm's way. He realized how much he cared for her, how much he wanted her in his life.

Moments later, James followed by Ralph, was led into the duke's study. Clarmont turned to them with a questioning look.

James explained the situation. The duke immediately rose to his feet.

"We will send for the Runners. However, we will not wait for them to arrive." He turned to his butler. "My brace of pistols if you please. And I want several sturdy footmen to accompany us as well."

"The carriage is waiting for us," Ralph said, a satisfied smile on his face.

James was impressed that the duke took charge so quickly. He rode inside the coach with the aristocrat while Ralph joined the coachman. Several young footmen were at the rear of the conveyance.

"Help yourself to any one of these weapons that catches your fancy," the duke told James.

"I am not knowledgeable in that regard."

"You did well enough with your fists against Foxworth," the duke said.

"Ordinarily, I deplore violence. However, I concede in some situations it proves necessary."

The duke gave him an approving nod. "Quite right."

They rode in silence for a time, each with his own thoughts. Eventually, the coach stopped moving and Ralph tapped the door.

"We're here," Ralph said.

"Good. Let us waste no more time. We need not wait for the Runners. They will arrive soon enough."

James followed the duke and Ralph, the two footmen behind him. Ralph used the knocker twice, got no response, and unceremoniously kicked open the door. The large man James had seen grab Brianna stood blocking their path, his muscled arms folded over his chest.

"What do you want here?" He virtually snarled at them.

"We have come for my sister who you have taken here against her will." The duke rose his quizzing glass and stared at the man as if he were vermin.

"Ain't no such person here."

Ralph stepped forward. "You got Miss Brianna and Fleur." He took an intimidating stance.

"No such thing."

Madam Louise sauntered across the vestibule. "You've got no call to come here. Those girls belong to me. Foxworth bought the one you call Brianna fair and square. She tricked me at first, but once Fleur said her name, I knew who she really was. I own her now. I got the document to prove it. Ogden signed over her guardianship for a fat sum. I was Foxworth's partner. So all this including the girls, now belongs to me. Here, read this for yourselves."

She held out the paper she claimed to be legally binding and thrust it forward.

The duke appeared undaunted. "That is an illegal document. I am my sister's guardian. Ogden never was. Now get my sister immediately or you will be brought before the magistrate."

"Bring Fleur as well," Ralph insisted. "She don't belong here either."

"Ha! She was one of my girls 'til the other one stole her from me." Louise's cheeks reddened. James thought the woman's ugly features appeared more porcine by the minute.

The duke pointed a pistol at her. "Send for both young ladies immediately." His voice was quiet but commanding.

Louise finally understood there would be no further discussion. She signaled her man.

"Tell Nell to get them and bring them down here."

The man grunted and left.

"I run a fine establishment here. Why I'll have you know Welly himself has come to visit the girls from time to time."

"I somehow doubt that," the duke said through gritted teeth.

They did not have long to wait. Both Brianna and Fleur were led downstairs. James was upset to see the side of Brianna's face was bruised. He came forward and took her into his arms.

The duke looked at her. "Are you all right?" he asked, genuine concern was expressed in his tone of voice.

She nodded. "Now that you have come to rescue us. I confess to feeling fear and confusion before."

"Downright panic," Fleur agreed. Ralph placed one arm around her, but kept his weapon pointed at Madam Louise. The duke did the same.

"We will leave this den of inequity forthwith," the duke said. He backed out the front door and the rest of them followed suit.

The ducal coach waited for them just outside the building. The duke turned to his sister.

"I am going to remain here until the Runners arrive. That should be very soon. In the meantime, I want you to return home. Have Maeve look at you. You appear injured. Maeve is a gifted healer among other things."

Brianna looked ready to protest. "You must come with us. It is dangerous to remain here."

"A Banbury tale. I am more than able to defend myself."

"Listen to me. There is something I have heard. Fleur and some of the other women here know the truth of what happened to Mr. Foxworth. He was murdered by Madam Louise. Is that not so, Fleur?"

All eyes turned to Fleur. "You should've not told, Miss. She'll have us killed, she will."

Brianna raised her chin. "You are wrong. She cannot hurt you or any of us. She will be arrested now, and you can give evidence in court."

"Ralph, get the women out of here," the duke said. "We will discuss this matter later."

James lifted Brianna and placed her in the carriage. Ralph did the same for Fleur. All the way back to Clarmont House, James held Brianna close. He never wanted to let go of her again.

CHAPTER FORTY-SEVEN

Brianna loved being held by James. It was comforting—no it was much more than that. She loved him. But he would expect a pure and innocent wife. Those words stuck painfully in her mind. He would expect something she was unable to provide. She freed herself from his embrace.

James did not leave when they arrived at Clarmont House as she had expected. He remained with her.

When the duke finally returned, he looked at Brianna's face and frowned. Her brother immediately sent for Maeve.

"Brianna has sustained some injuries. Please look at her and see if I should send for a physician to examine her."

Maeve studied her face. "I know you are in some pain," she said. "Come with me and we shall see what can be done."

Brianna nodded. But first, she turned to Fleur. "You must speak up and tell the magistrate what Louise did. I believe the other women can be convinced to do the same if you go forward."

Fleur bit her lower lip. "It ain't that easy, Miss."

Ralph placed his arms around her. "I won't let nothing happen to you. You're going to be my wife. I protect what's mine. You have my word." His voice was fierce and raw with emotion.

Fleur responded, "All right. I suppose I can—as long as you're with me, Ralph."

"That's my girl!" he said, responding with a hug and quick kiss. "We won't let that vulture hurt no one else again."

"You do not need to fear that wretched woman," the duke agreed. "You are under my protection as well. You did see the madam murder Foxworth, did you not?"

"Oh, yes, Your Grace, I did indeed. He were lying there on the ground dazed from this fellow giving him a facer. After Mr. Winthrop left the alleyway, she come out. I suppose Louise was watching what happened. We all was if truth be told. Anyway, she picks up this big rock that's part of the decoration there and smashes Mr. Foxworth over the noggin with it. Well, I don't know if that was what killed him. But for good measure, she took his knife and plunged it into his body. It were a grim sight. Then she come back to the house. She gathered us all together and said we was never to tell anyone what we seen and if we did, well the same thing that happened to Mr. Foxworth would happen to us. I always knew Madam Louise was mean, but I didn't know she could kill someone. She took over running the house afterwards like she owned it. No one was going to gainsay her." Fleur shuddered.

"Fleur needs to rest after her ordeal," Maeve said. "I will send my maid to you." Maeve turned to Brianna. "I want to look you over right now. We will wash the wound clean and then I have an excellent salve to put on it."

Maeve took her arm and led Brianna upstairs. Being in her sister-in-law's capable hands made her feel better already. As they ascended the staircase, she overheard James ask her brother if they might speak in private.

~♥~

JAMES WAS ON edge, but he realized that he must approach the duke regarding his intentions toward Brianna. Although he felt confused about what her feelings toward him were, James believed it was time to speak to His Grace. Perhaps that was what Brianna wanted him to do before their relationship could be more serious in nature.

"You wish to talk with me, young man?" the duke said. His manner was as haughty as ever.

James refused to be intimidated. He had much to offer any young woman. He followed the duke to his study. The duke shut the door and turned to James.

"What matter is so pressing that you feel it must be discussed at such a time?" Obviously, His Grace was not pleased by James' request.

He cleared his throat. “I should like to pay my addresses to your sister, Your Grace.”

“Is she aware of this?”

James swallowed. His mouth felt as if cotton had been stuffed in it. “Yes, she is aware.”

“And has she encouraged you in this declaration?”

“I believe so.”

The duke stared at him. “She has not told me anything of it.”

James folded his hands behind his back, bracing himself. “I believe she might have shared some information with your wife.”

The duke studied him further. “I see. You do understand that Brianna has just entered society. I feel she will have many offers.”

“I truly love her, and I believe she loves me.”

“Very well, I will have a word with her, and we will talk again on this matter. You must understand that I do not wish to dictate to my sister. As it happens, she is a woman of strong character and will make her own decisions. I intend to bestow upon her a generous portion that many men would covet.”

“Your Grace, I do not need nor want any form of dowry. Anything you wish to provide would be kept in Brianna’s name alone.”

“Unusual but commendable,” the duke said approvingly.

“Thank you, Your Grace.”

“You may court my sister if you wish.” He offered a dismissive movement of his hand.

James left Clarmont House feeling lighter in spirit. He intended a vigorous pursuit of Brianna.

BRIANNA CONTINUED TO receive many invitations, more than she was willing or eager to accept. Gwen leaned over her shoulder as she was sorting them.

“You are so popular, my lady. All the maids agree you are a great success. Are you excited?”

Brianna shrugged, not certain just how to answer that. It took several days for her to recover from her ordeal. Maeve gave her willow bark tea for the pain and that helped, but Brianna was feeling out of sorts. It was because of James, she realized. She wondered what he must think of her. Still, he had been there when she needed him.

She decided to speak again with Maeve. Visiting her sister-in-law was always a delight when Maggie was present. Maeve had just finished nursing her daughter and the nanny took the baby to get ready for a nap.

"Is this a bad time for a chat?" Brianna asked hesitantly.

Maeve smiled, "Not at all. What do you wish to talk about?"

"Can you not guess?"

"Would it be James Winthrop?"

Brianna nodded.

"He has come each afternoon since the abduction. You have not chosen to see him."

Brianna sat down on a chair. "I have not been up to making polite conversation."

"Coward!"

"I take umbrage to your accusation."

"Do you, even if it happens to be true?"

"All right," she conceded. "I have not known what to say to him."

Maeve came to her. "Just speak from your heart, my dear. Be honest and truthful. If he is the right man for you, it will become apparent from his response. You have courage. Apply it now."

Brianna licked her lips. "You make it sound so simple."

"Because it is. Trust me."

Brianna hoped that was true. "All right. I will speak to him directly."

Maeve beamed. "Good. It is for the best."

Brianna reached into the pocket of her skirt and removed Maeve's necklace. "I am returning this to you. I confess I forgot to wear it on the day Fleur and I were kidnapped. It was a mistake. But I believe I am safe now."

"You are welcome to wear it as long as you like," Maeve said.

Brianna shook her head. "No, it belongs with you and someday it will be Maggie's."

"Let us make a plan," Maeve said. "Send James an invitation to tea tomorrow. We will welcome no other guests at that time. I will see to it that you and Mr. Winthrop have some private time to speak."

"A good plan," Brianna agreed.

That afternoon, there were many visitors including James. Lord Randall was particularly solicitous of her well-being. James looked discouraged.

"So happy to see you in looks," Lord Randall said. "Though you do seem a bit pale. What an exciting life you lead."

Brianna lowered her eyes, not knowing how to respond to his comment.

"Howard, we are doing our best to put the incident out of our minds," Maeve said.

He inclined his head. "Of course, perfectly reasonable. Perhaps you will honor me with a ride through the park?"

"What a splendid idea," Maeve said.

Brianna looked over at James, but he said nothing, merely appearing dejected.

"Yes, I would like that. I have not been out in days."

"Do you much good," Lord Randall said.

"Mr. Winthrop and I can have some time for a chat in the meantime," Maeve said. She offered Brianna a meaningful glance.

Brianna sent for Gwen who brought her pelisse and bonnet. The three of them set out for a drive in the park. She was pleased to see that Lord Randall had thoughtfully brought a Landau drawn by a pair of silky bays. The conveyance had room for her maid to sit with them in comfort.

In the presence of her maid, they merely discussed the usual banalities, talk of the weather, how pleased the duke and duchess were with the progress of their baby, and what entertainments were of interest in the city.

"I like your vehicle," Brianna said.

"Yes, I thought you would. It is comfortable. Just the right sort to see and be seen on Rotten Row. Perhaps a brief walk along the Serpentine?"

Brianna nodded. She did love to walk along the water. She missed the lakes in Switzerland which were far more scenic, but this would have to do. She wondered fleetingly if she would ever be able to return there and visit her school.

Lord Randall turned to Gwen. "Perhaps you would prefer to remain in the carriage? It is growing chilly. I have warm bricks for your feet."

Her maid smiled appreciatively at his consideration. "Thank you, your lordship."

"That was kind of you," Brianna said as they began walking.

"Nothing of the sort. I merely wished to be alone with you for a bit. I wanted to ask how you are really doing."

"Much better. Thank you for asking. And thank you for the flowers each day."

He waved his hand. "A mere trifle. You deserve much more. I am aware you have and will have many suitors. I wish to be counted among them."

She turned and looked at him. He was in the first stare of fashion from his artfully arranged a la Brutus hairstyle to his gleaming Hessians polished to mirror perfection.

"May I ask you a question?"

He smiled at her. "Anything at all, fair lady."

She hesitated but then decided to throw caution to the wind. "I have been wondering why men think their brides must be pure maidens while the women accept that men who are well-experienced are desirable."

Lord Randall tugged uncomfortably at his collar. It had not been a question he was expecting. "I suppose it is just the way of the world. The way things are." He shrugged.

"But why must we accept that?"

He turned away. "Ah, there are geese and some ducks. I am sorry I did not think to bring something to feed them."

Brianna understood her question would not be answered by him, not today, probably not ever. However, just the same, she did not regret asking it.

THE FOLLOWING MORNING, Gwen helped her dress. Her maid was in high spirits. "Would you like me to try dressing your hair in the latest style I seen of late?"

"No, thank you, Gwen. I like the new short lengths, but I prefer keeping it simple."

Gwen gave her a doubtful look. "Lord Randall is a fashionable gent. I thought maybe you'd like to look more stylish."

Brianna was finding her maid annoying. "I do not feel the need to impress him."

Gwen looked abashed. "Sorry, just want to be helpful. I've heard it said that Lord Randall is plump in the pockets, almost as well off as His Grace. And he does seem very interested in you."

"Thank you, Gwen. I will likely need you later." She dismissed her maid without further comment.

Was she interested in Lord Randall romantically? She did not think so. When she saw James, her feelings were entirely different. Her heart beat faster. But Maeve was right, she must speak with him openly and honestly. She could not marry him otherwise. Still, she dreaded it.

THAT AFTERNOON, JAMES did come. He had responded to Maeve's invitation. Her sister-in-law had given instructions that no one else was to be received. Specifically, visitors could leave their cards, but the family was officially not at home this afternoon to visitors. Only Mr. Winthrop was to be shown into the drawing room.

Maeve was already ordering tea when Brianna joined her and James. Maeve chatted with him in a pleasant, friendly manner. Brianna spoke very little. She avoided making eye contact with James. She was polite but distant. Finally, after the amenities were done, Maeve rose from her chair.

"I must check on Maggie. I think it is time for her next feeding. If you both will excuse me. I believe you have some matters to discuss." Maeve made a point of shutting the drawing room doors as she left the room.

They were quite alone now. Brianna heard the ticking of the clock. James rose and drew near her.

"I assume you wish to talk with me," he said.

She nodded. This was terribly difficult. "I have something important to tell you."

He appeared alarmed. "Are you refusing my proposal? When you accepted and then ran out, I had to assume that something I said or did made you change your mind. But I have not changed my mind. You should know my feelings for you are sincere."

She bit her lower lip. "Please take a seat again. It occurred to me that we hardly know each other. There are things you must know, must be able to accept before I can in good conscience marry you."

He came and sat down next to her, taking her hands in his own. "Darling, I love you. There is nothing you could tell me that will change that."

She removed her hands from his and shook her head. "I am not convinced of that." She took a deep breath and let it out slowly. "I must begin by saying that my mother was nothing like yours."

"I gathered as much," he said with a wry smile.

"She loved being admired by men. All through my childhood, we traveled. She was a restless soul, never satisfied to be in one place for very long. She had more than one lover. When I was eleven, she was the mistress of a very wealthy man. He ravished me one night."

"How horrible!" James was clearly shocked by her confession.

"It was. Mama blamed me. She said I had somehow enticed him. She broke off her affair with him, but that was when she decided to put me in school and keep me away from her. It was for the best. But you see now why I cannot accept your proposal. You expect a bride that is pure and innocent. I am neither." She looked up and their eyes met.

James shook his head. "You are still pure and innocent. You must not think otherwise. Truth be told, I may not be good enough for you."

Brianna was surprised by his statement. "I do not understand."

He took her hands in his again. "I had not wanted to ever marry because I felt the illness that afflicted my father would be passed down to me. The doctor explained that it was hereditary you see. When my mother and I finally discussed the matter, she had a confession of her own. I was not my father's natural child. My mother was *enceinte* when they married. He knew all about it. My birth father had died and could not marry her. My adopted father was happy to have a son. Like me, he did not intend to father children himself. So you see, technically I was born on the wrong side of the blanket so to speak. Does that change your opinion of me?"

"Not in the slightest. I love you and think you are quite wonderful."

"Good enough to marry the sister of a duke?"

"Too good."

They shared a laugh together. James took her into his arms and kissed her with tenderness and reverence.

"I promise to make you happy, to always treat you with the love and respect you deserve."

Brianna found herself crying. James looked alarmed.

"Did I say something wrong again?" he asked.

She shook her head, overcome by emotion. "No, not at all. What you said was wonderful. Please come for dinner tonight with your mother. We can make the announcement together then."

James agreed. They kissed again, this time more passionately. Brianna thought this was the most perfect moment of her life.

CHAPTER FORTY-EIGHT

BRIANNA HELD HANDS WITH JAMES as they announced their betrothal to the family that evening. They gathered in the drawing room before dinner, the duke, Maeve, and Anna Winthrop, a small group but all that really mattered. Maeve and Anna were both excited but expressed their pleasure in different ways. Anna broke down and cried while Maeve hugged and kissed Brianna and James.

The duke was much more reserved. "I wish you happiness," he said.

"Thank you, Your Grace. I will do everything in my power to make your sister happy."

"I do not doubt it."

"We are both fortunate," Brianna said quickly.

"I have always wanted a daughter and now I shall have one," Anna said offering her own hugs.

"What about a Christmas wedding?" Maeve asked. "Or would that be too soon?"

Brianna looked over at James. "I would have no problem with that. I want a small wedding, just family. No fuss or bother."

"And I was thinking of a large ton wedding in June," the duke said. "It would be appropriate."

"Not for me," Brianna said. "I only want a few people who really matter to us in attendance."

"We have another wedding to plan as well," Maeve said, quickly changing the subject to avoid argument.

"Oh, and whose would that be?" the duke asked, raising one gold-tipped eyebrow.

"Ralph and Fleur, of course," Maeve replied. "They are getting married as well. Ralph has informed me that when he told Mr. Brockton, our benefactor insisted that the wedding breakfast be at his townhouse. Brianna and I will help plan it naturally."

The duke shrugged. "I suppose that is appropriate."

"Indeed. Ralph is returning to his employment very soon."

"Now that is good news," the duke said. He finally managed to smile.

Maeve laughed and smacked his hand.

Dinner was a pleasant affair. She and James were toasted by her brother a bit excessively. But she felt he was trying for her sake to accept her bourgeois fiancé, and Brianna did appreciate it. She was well aware that her brother looked down on those engaged in trade as inferiors.

VISITING MR. Brockton's townhouse with Maeve and Maggie was an adventure considering all the baggage and people involved on such a short trip. The maid and nanny were part of the entourage. The duke insisted on two footmen as a bare minimum of protection.

Mr. Brockton's home was much cozier than the ducal residence, but it was nicely furnished and in good taste. Maeve's benefactor as she liked to call him was a jovial host. When Brianna commented on the attractiveness of his home, Mr. Brockton's face lit up.

"It was all Maeve's doing. And she brought me Mary and Ginny who keep everything running tip-top." Mr. Brockton then sent for the two women he had mentioned.

Both Mary and Ginny were young, probably only a few years older than Brianna. They both greeted Maeve with warmth. The planning for Ralph and Fleur's wedding was accomplished in record time. It was decided that they would be married by Common License.

Mr. Brockton would pay the fee to the local clergyman and Ralph and Fleur could be married within fifteen days.

"Happens I have an estate in the country now," Mr. Brockton explained. "It has a main house and a nice guest cottage on the premises. I am going to give the cottage to Ralph. He and his wife can live there when they choose."

"Very generous," Maeve said. She looked at him askance. "Since when did you purchase a country home?"

He looked down at the carpet. "I might have engaged in a bit of gambling. And I might just have won the estate from an unlucky fellow."

Maeve stood abruptly. "I thought we agreed that you would only run your gambling establishment and no longer gamble yourself." Her manner was stern.

"Now, my dear girl, I rarely do so anymore. This game was just too tempting. And I won, didn't I?"

Maeve folded her arms over her chest, her expression formidable. "You could lose everything if you are not careful. I want your word you will not gamble again."

Mr. Brockton let out a deep sigh. "Very well," he said. "You've taken the pleasure out of it for me. You are a termagant."

"Only when necessary."

Maggie woke from sleep and began to cry.

"Let me look at her," Mr. Brockton said, eager to change the subject.

Maeve lifted the baby and brought her to him.

"She's a beauty, just like her mother." The mood in the room lightened. Mr. Brockton held out his arms and Maeve allowed him to hold her child.

Ralph and Fleur entered the room hand in hand. Fleur looked younger and sweeter with the make-up washed from her face. Ralph, although much older than Fleur, seemed transformed as well.

"The ladies have been planning your wedding," Mr. Brockton told Ralph and Fleur.

"Do not go to much trouble for us," Ralph said. He appeared embarrassed.

But Fleur seemed pleased. She beamed at everyone. "This is all so grand," she said. "You have all been so kind. I feel like a princess in a fairy tale. Thank you." She burst into tears.

THE PLANNING FOR Brianna's wedding was more complex, mainly because the duke insisted on being involved.

"Your marriage can proceed after the posting of the Banns," the duke informed Brianna. "Your names will be read in church for three consecutive Sundays and will also be posted. Then you may marry. I prefer St. George's Parish

Church. It is in the heart of Mayfair and is where the fashionable people are married."

"But I am not fashionable nor is James."

Her brother sighed deeply. "Must you always be difficult? Grant me this one allowance."

Maeve gave her a nod.

"Yes, Your Grace, as you wish."

He touched her cheek with his fingertips. "I think you should start calling me Adam. We are blood relations after all."

She smiled at her brother. "Very well." A sense of relief washed over her as she finally felt accepted.

SINCE RALPH AND Fleur's wedding was before her own, Brianna was selected as maid of honor. The small church chosen for the ceremony comfortably accommodated the wedding party which consisted of Brianna and James, Maeve, Mr. Brockton, Mary and Ginny, Charles and Caroline, and several of the young women from the brothel.

Brianna thought Ralph and Fleur looked indeed happy and in love. Afterwards, they celebrated at Mr. Brockton's home.

"I can hardly wait until it is our turn," Brianna told James.

He kissed her hand, first peeling back her glove. "I cannot wait for our wedding either."

Caroline observed them. "Another wedding soon. How romantic!"

The girls from Fleur's former employment gathered around her. They were deep in conversation when Fleur called Brianna to join them.

"You'll want to know about this. Your young man will as well."

Brianna took James' hand, and they joined the young women.

"Nell has taken over the duties of running the house," Fleur told them.

"What has happened to Louise? We have not been told," Brianna said.

"She's being transported. She won't hang after all. The authorities are sending her to Botany Bay on the next ship out."

"Good riddance I say," one of the other girls said with a sneer.

There was general agreement.

"Mark my words, she'll start her business there soon enough," Fleur said.

The other young woman who had spoken before nodded in agreement. "I hear there's a shortage of women prisoners but plenty of men."

Brianna did not comment. She was grateful to see the last of Madam Louise and wanted to forget the entire incident as much as it was possible.

CHAPTER FORTY-NINE

BRIANNA WAS NERVOUS ON THE morning of her wedding. It had snowed the night before and she looked out her bedroom window and saw the world covered in beauty. The sun came out and it was as if nature were providing her with the perfect morning to be wed. It was a good omen, she decided.

Gwen brought her hot chocolate, and she drank what she could. But her stomach was fluttering as if butterflies were present in it.

"I'll help you dress," Gwen said.

Brianna agreed. Still, she waited a little longer. She was relieved when Maeve joined her.

"I am doing the right thing, do you not think?" Brianna turned a questioning look on Maeve.

"Do you love James?"

"With all my heart."

"Then of course you are doing the right thing in marrying him. There are no guarantees in life but starting out in marriage with someone you love is the best thing to do. I know many marry for money, convenience, or position, but I do not consider that best."

Brianna nodded. She was of a similar opinion.

"You married my brother because you loved him, did you not?"

"Most certainly," Maeve agreed. "We are very different people, but somehow, we complete each other. There is no one else I would want to spend my life with but him."

Gwen brought out her wedding gown. She had chosen green satin with several red flounces and ruffles to celebrate the Christmas season. She was tired of wearing white and pale pastel colors. Today she would be a vibrant bride. Her bridal gown was a perfection of the French dressmaking art, rich satin with seed pearls overlaying the bodice and shot through with silver threads. Her hair was dressed to flatter with small, soft curls framing her heart-shaped face.

~♥~

BRIANA AND HER brother had come to an accord. The wedding breakfast would be limited to an intimate gathering with a guest list approved by herself and James while they would in turn be married at the church chosen by the duke.

Saint George's Church in Hanover Square was decorated appropriately for the Christmas wedding. There were red and white poinsettias along the aisles. Brianna's own bouquet was composed of red roses obtained from a hothouse and quite a luxury at this time of year. Her brother had ordered it. Maeve, as matron of honor, also had a bouquet of red roses which fit nicely with the deep maroon of her satin gown.

Brianna stood in an alcove at the back of the church, her brother next to her.

"You are a beautiful bride," he said. "Before it is time for us to march down the aisle, there are two matters I feel it necessary to mention to you."

She offered a questioning look. What could he possibly wish to discuss at such a time?

"First, you should know that I am settling a large portion on you. Your bridegroom has refused to accept it. He wishes that what is given be solely in your name. He has told me that he has no need for any form of dowry. In that respect he is unusual. Perhaps you have chosen well," her brother conceded.

Brianna smiled. His approval may have been given grudgingly, but at least it was finally offered. "What was the second thing you wished to tell me?"

The duke suddenly pulled at his collar. "This is not an easy matter to discuss, but it must be said. I did not invite your mother to the wedding. I made no attempt to locate her."

Brianna nodded, accepting what he said. "I did not either. She is not just my mother. She is yours as well. However, I do not wish this special day to be marred by bad feelings. Be not perturbed." She placed her hand on his sleeve. "You have done well by me, Adam."

He looked pleased at her use of his given name. It implied affection and understanding between them.

"I should have provided you with a piece of family jewelry. However, our mother took all the valuable jewels with her when she left here."

"I really do not need them," Brianna said.

The organ music began. The duke stiffened in readiness. From her vantage point, she saw James slowly start down the aisle. His mother's hand was on his arm as they walked side by side. He had chosen his mother rather than the traditional best man. How thoughtful of James. He looked dashing in formal black attire, snowy shirt and tie. Maeve followed walking down the aisle by herself. Then it was the bride's turn. Her hand was on her brother's arm. Those in attendance rose to their feet. Organ music reverberated. It was a wonderful moment.

Maeve took her bouquet to hold. Her brother stepped to one side beside his wife. The service itself went by quickly. She felt dazed and hoped she answered correctly. James placed the wedding band on her finger. They kissed sweetly to much applause. Marching back down the aisle hand in hand, she and James accepted congratulations from all those present. Brianna's hand trembled slightly with emotion when she signed the registry, realizing that this truly was the most momentous occasion in her life.

As they left the church, rice was thrown over them. Both she and James laughed, enjoying the tradition.

The carriage James had provided was elegant and drawn by two white horses.

"We can take the long way back to Clarmont House if you like," James told her.

Brianna nodded. "I should like that greatly." She smiled at him.

For a time, they clung to each other. Brianna looked at her handsome husband and marveled that this was true, and she was really married to James.

"Mrs. Winthrop I would like to kiss you again." James leaned over her.

"I do wish you would," she said.

James took her right hand in his and slowly removed her glove. He proceeded to kiss, lick, and then suck each finger. It felt strangely erotic. Next, he kissed her forehead, then her lips.

He trailed kisses down her neck to her throat and then opened her cape to gently lower the bodice of her gown. Her exposed flesh goose-bumped in the chilly coach. But James found the remedy for that by sucking on first one nipple and then the other. Brianna moaned with aroused desire.

James quickly covered her again. "No more of this or I shall embarrass myself by losing all control. Later," he said, "that is a promise."

"One we shall both keep," she said, adjusting the bodice of her gown.

They shared a chaste kiss and smiled into each other's eyes as the coach stopped in front of the ducal residence.

"Ready to greet our guests?" James asked.

Brianna took a deep breath and then slowly let it out. "Absolutely," she replied.

Hand in hand they entered the great house where the main rooms were festively decorated for both the wedding and the season. Maeve and the duke greeted them and then led them into the drawing room where the guests were gathered.

Lord Randall was the first to shake James' hand. In contrast to his homely features, he was dressed in his usual fashionably elaborate manner. "Lucky fellow," he said to James. "I wanted to offer for her, but her heart was clearly elsewhere. May I kiss the bride?"

"That is entirely her decision," James said.

Brianna offered her cheek. Smiling, Lord Randall gave her a chaste peck. He moved to the other side of the room and allowed Charles and Caroline to congratulate them.

"This is so romantic," Caroline rhapsodized. "A Christmas wedding symbolizes new life. Your life together is just beginning. Charles, do you not think it is grand?"

Charles smiled down at his wife. "I am certain you are right." He leaned over to stage whisper in James' ear. "Take warning. This is what happens when a man marries. We become docile and agree with whatever our wives say."

Caroline's face flushed with indignation. "That is untrue. Absolute rubbish. Really, Charles, such moonshine."

Her husband merely laughed. Not the most sensitive of men surely, Brianna decided.

Still, they seemed happy together and Caroline was clearly increasing.

The Duke of Rundwall was next to offer his good wishes. He looked pale and thin. Her brother had mentioned that he was in poor health.

Brianna noticed that James was looking around. When his eyes lit on his mother, his spine stiffened. He turned to Brianna.

"There is a matter I must take care of before we go to the dining room. You must excuse me, darling."

"Of course."

Brianna watched as James strode across the room to his mother and took her hands in his. She in turn looked troubled. What could be the problem?

CHAPTER FIFTY

"MOTHER, THERE IS SOMETHING I must tell you."

Anna looked at her son with a penetrating gaze. "I believe I already know."

"Then I truly must explain." He held her hand and led her to a quiet corner of the room. "When you finally trusted me with the information of your past, I asked Brianna's brother to help me locate your family. He has connections. It was not difficult as it turned out to discover the whereabouts of your sisters. They all three married and are still living in Sussex. I obtained their addresses, wrote to them, told them of our connection, and invited them to the wedding."

His mother looked upset. "You should have consulted me first before doing such a thing."

"And what would you have said?"

"I would have refused naturally."

"That is why I did not tell you. First, I wanted to wait for their responses. They all three accepted. They are here. They were at the church sitting toward the rear. I believe they have just arrived. I asked the butler to signal me and he has. Please join me in greeting them."

He took his mother's hand again and resolutely placed it on his arm, then walked her toward the front hall. There standing on the marble floor under the large chandelier were three well-dressed ladies, somewhat younger than his mother and bearing a clear resemblance. Each had dark hair and brown eyes. They looked around, clearly impressed by their surroundings.

It took some time, but introductions were made. The tallest and oldest of the three women acted as spokesperson.

"Anna, when your son wrote to us, we were overwhelmed by emotion. For years we wondered what happened to you and where you might be. Quite frankly, we feared the worst.

Mama was heartbroken. You were her favorite. She died two years later. She never forgave Papa. He was a cruel man. His behavior was unforgivable. He took a second wife and had a son by her who eventually became the baronet. I am Josephine, Josie, in case you do not remember me. I look rather different now I daresay."

The other two sisters stepped forward. "I am Fredrica." She had a sweet voice and smile.

"And I am Celia. I was very little when you left."

"I hope we may be sisters again. We mourned your loss." Josie opened her arms.

Anna started to weep and allowed herself to be hugged by each of her sisters in turn. It was an emotional moment for them. James was relieved that this reconciliation had gone so well. He had not been certain it would, but he had hoped.

"We left our families to come to London and join this celebration. I hope we did not overstep," Fredrica said.

"No, I am glad you are here. I have missed my family," his mother said. "We have much to catch up on."

Anna's three sisters surrounded and embraced her warmly. James stepped away wanting to allow the sisters a private moment before joining the rest of the company. He had taken a risk, but it proved worthwhile. He had a feeling his mother would never feel lonely again.

JAMES REJOINED HIS wife. Brianna threw him a questioning look.

"I will explain later. I promise you will be pleased."

Brianna was curious as to what had happened. Why was James being secretive?

Maeve spoke up. "We must all go into the dining room and enjoy the excellent wedding breakfast our cook and her helpers have prepared for us."

The duke took his wife's arm and led the way. Her brother and sister-in-law were seated first at the head of the long table. James was then seated next to her brother while Brianna was seated beside Maeve. The Duke of Rundwall, as the most important guest, was seated next to James. Beside him was Charles who was Rundwall's heir and now a marquess. On Charles' other side, Mr. Brockton, Charles' other father was seated. That too seemed appropriate. Caroline was seated beside Brianna and next to her was Anna Winthrop. Then there were three ladies she did not recognize. They appeared to know Mrs. Winthrop. She assumed they were invited by James or his mother.

Ralph and Fleur were not present. Maeve had told her they were out in the country looking over Mr. Brockton's new estate. Perhaps Ralph would wish to retire there to the cottage Mr. Brockton was giving him as a marriage gift and for his many years of devotion and service.

Another person missing that she made note of was Lord Randall. Brianna turned to Maeve.

"Did Lord Randall leave?"

Maeve nodded. "I am afraid so. He offered his apologies to Adam, but claimed he had a pressing engagement."

"I do hope I have not hurt his feelings."

Maeve touched her hand. "Howard is not all that sensitive. He will quickly recover. Do not concern yourself. This is your special day. You and James must enjoy yourselves."

Brianna's attention was drawn to her brother who was now raising a glass of champagne to toast herself and James. There were numerous toasts followed by a sumptuous meal which seemed to stretch on too long. But the final toast touched her deeply.

Anna Winthrop stood up. She looked self-conscious but raised her glass with determination. "Brianna has brought joy to both my life and that of my son. I think of her as a daughter." Brianna saw the tears and sincerity in her mother-in-law's eyes. She was moved but found herself without words.

CHAPTER FIFTY-ONE

FINALLY, THE GUESTS DEPARTED, AND Brianna was able to spend time alone with James.

"Are your bags packed?" he asked.

"Not entirely. James, you have not told me where we are going. I thought perhaps you might want to spend our first night together here in my room."

He shook his head. "No, I think that would be a bad idea."

"Your house?"

He again shook his head. "There are going to be house guests there."

"Let me guess. Those three ladies sitting with your mother?"

He smiled. "They are her sisters, now reunited after a lifetime apart."

"And let me guess again. You arranged it," Brianna said.

He laughed. "You already know me too well."

"Why did you not tell me before? Was it some sort of mystery?"

He held her hands in his own. "I did not know if it would be possible. I was not certain until the other day. It is a great pleasure to see them together. We will visit with them, but not tonight."

"So where are we to go? Is this another secret?"

"Not at all. I have made reservations for us at one of the finest hotels in London. It is called The Pulteney. It is located at the west corner of Bolton Street in Piccadilly. I have engaged their best rooms for the next few days. We shall have our privacy."

Brianna laughed. James seemed so proud of himself.

"And will we need privacy?" she said in a teasing voice.

"I certainly hope so," James responded. "And when the weather turns warm again, I plan for us to take a trip to Brighton. I fancy some sea air."

"That sounds wonderful."

"So now get that bag packed. I am eager to begin our adventure together." He gave her a smacking kiss which she returned with enthusiasm.

~♥~

THE HOTEL WAS elegant and the most expensive in London. Brianna was duly impressed with their accommodation. Their suite of rooms faced the mews which was somewhat quieter than the front street. But noise in no way occupied her mind. The thought of finally being alone with James thrilled her senses.

"I will give you time to unpack and then come back later," James said. "Would you like to have a maid sent to you to help?"

"No, I can manage." Brianna never had a maid when she was in school. She had learned to make do for herself. That, of course, was not the case at the Winthrop house or the ducal mansion.

Gwen had been there to help remove her wedding dress with all the tiny buttons down the back. But Brianna had chosen her trousseau with care, only simple clothing that would not need a maid's attention. Like James, she wanted privacy for their first days together. She also knew that James did not employ a personal valet as most gentlemen did. It was another of the things she admired about him. He was a man of independent spirit.

Brianna removed the night rail Maeve had given her as a bride's gift from her baggage. It was a white satin gown nearly translucent and in the Grecian style. The high-waisted bodice made the most of her small breasts and the gown emphasized her slim waist.

Brianna pulled out her hairbrush and tortoise shell combs. She brushed her dark blonde hair until it gleamed and caught the light like gold guineas. Then she set the combs to lift back the mass. She examined her appearance in the looking glass and decided she looked her best. She might not have a voluptuous figure, but it was still attractive. She hoped James would find her so. She was nervous but not as much as she had feared she would be.

A knock sounded at the door. James called out. “May I enter?”

“Please do,” she returned.

He studied her with apparent pleasure. “You are a goddess,” he said. Then he swept her into his arms. “I am the most fortunate of men.”

“And I am the luckiest of ladies,” she replied.

They embraced. Then James lifted her into his arms and carried her toward a comfortable chair. She was surprised, expecting that he would want to immediately take her to bed. However, James set her down, seated himself on the chair, and then lifted her onto his lap.

“Are you happy?” he asked her, cuddling her close.

“Very happy,” she said, smiling into his dark brown eyes, so like hot chocolate.

“I am glad. I want us to have a good life together now and always.” He leaned forward and kissed her ardently.

She loved the taste of him. His kiss was like a heady liqueur, full of sweetness and spice. She kissed him back eagerly. His lips moved from hers to her neck and down the swell of her breasts. He gently lowered her gown and then kissed, licked, and sucked each of her nipples in turn. Her nipples tightened and hardened. She moaned in his arms. She had never felt such incredible pleasure. There was heat between her legs. She felt something stirring within herself and him as well.

James lifted her from the chair and carried her to the large bed in the center of the room.

He placed her there as if she were a fragile, valuable sculpture. He came over her and kissed his way down her body, gently lifting and removing her gown. Then he began kissing his way to the special place between her legs that was becoming wet with anticipation.

An energy hummed between them. An awareness. His eyes locked seductively on hers. He lifted each of her hands to his lips and kissed each finger. His hands then ran down her sides with caresses so sensual she moaned. His mouth came down on hers in a hot, moist rush. She opened her lips to his heat. The heat and intimacy of their embrace was not enough. She longed with desire to meld herself with him, that they become one. His tongue caressed and licked her lips with liquid fire.

One hand reached up to caress and then cup her breasts. He rubbed her bottom. His hand moved to fondle the soft, hidden flesh between her legs just as his kisses had done before. She was mad with desire for him. When he entered her, she was not afraid. She welcomed him. His member was large, but it did not hurt her. She refused to think of the past, of what had once happened to her. This was different. She was with James. He was devoted to bringing her pleasure, to worshipping her body.

The pulsing rhythm between them grew stronger and intensified until something happened to her. She felt as if she had fractured into a thousand myriad pieces. She thought she would fly apart. A shivering, shuddering convulsive sense of release swept through her. She was still quivering with aftershocks when he drove himself deeply into her hot, wet tightness and surrendered to his own climax. Her body convulsed around him and was caught up in the throes of rapture. She could scarcely breathe.

"I love you," he said in a breathless whisper as they finally came apart.

"James, I love you too," she said.

For a long time, they lay in each other's arms. No other words seemed needed.

CHAPTER FIFTY-TWO

THEY BREAKFASTED HUNGRILY THE FOLLOWING morning. It had been an exciting night, one of pleasure and learning what pleased each other. She felt like an explorer who had come to a new world. Although she was a bit sore, it hardly mattered.

James sent for their breakfast to be served in the sitting room. She thought there ought to be words between them, meaningful ones. But they were ravenous and so eating occupied them for some time.

"The poached eggs are delicious," Brianna said.

James agreed as he spread marmalade on his toast. They shared a pot of coffee as they smiled into each other's eyes. When they were both satiated, James gazed at her thoughtfully.

"I hope what we did together last night was satisfying, that is, I hope I did not discomfort or disappoint you." He lowered his eyes as if embarrassed to make such a statement.

"Not at all," she reassured him, placing her hand over his on the table.

"I believed it was wrong for me to indulge in such a manner. You understand I believed that my father's illness would be passed to me and then any child I might father. For that reason, I had decided to lead a life that was celibate." His eyes did not meet her own. "I am aware that men are expected to be at least somewhat experienced in such things."

"I think it good that at least one of us was a virgin," she said with a wry smile.

Now he looked up. “But you were a virgin in every way that matters,” he said with sincerity. “Has a man ever made love to you before?”

She shook her head.

“I knew that was the case. I am grateful that you did not let your first encounter with a man, horrible as it was, destroy your ability to find pleasure with me. I am humbled by your courage.”

“James, it was wonderful with you. I love you so much.”

They moved away from the table and embraced.

“We will learn about the physical side of lovemaking together,” James said. “Make no mistake, you are innocent and pure.”

Brianna knew that James was the right man for her, that they would spend their lives together, helping and loving each other.

THE END

NOTES FROM THE AUTHOR

I THOUGHT I SHOULD PROVIDE a brief discussion of how this novel came about. When I wrote *Tea Leaves and Tarot Cards,* the novel was originally published by Five Star/ Cengage in both a hardcover edition and a hardcover large print edition. Because of positive reviews, it was widely ordered by libraries including my local library. One of the librarians there loved the book and told all of her friends to read it. She urged me to write a sequel on more than one occasion. Other readers who also liked the book had one complaint. They believed I must write Brianna's story. I was not ready at that time. But since then, *Tea Leaves* has had both paperback and ebook editions. The requests have continued.

And so I finally began writing *The Lost Lady*. This Regency novel continues where *Tea Leaves* left off. I enjoyed writing it and hope you as readers will enjoy it as well. It was a labor of love.

For those who are interested, here is my blog information: http://jacquelineseewald.blogspot.com

Best to all of you,

Jacqueline Seewald

A BRIEF NOTE FOR PURISTS AND STICKLERS FOR HISTORICAL ACCURACY

I TOOK SOME LIBERTIES WITH the history of the era. Although the Elgin Marbles were in London in 1816, they were not displayed to the public at the British Museum until 1817. Lord Byron among others attacked Lord Elgin for removing these art treasures from Greece. A debate had ensued in Parliament.

James Winthrop's adoptive father would have suffered from Huntington's Disease, but at the time the hereditary neuro-degenerative ailment was yet to be named. That would not occur until much later in the century.

ALSO BY JACQUELINE SEEWALD

Dark Moon Rising

Sinful Seduction

Highland Heart

Tea Leaves and Tarot Cards

The Killing Land

REVIEWS FOR TEA LEAVES AND TAROT CARDS

"*JACQUELINE SEEWALD'S TEA Leaves and Tarot Cards delivers an unusual and intriguing heroine together with fast-paced historical romantic-suspense. Seewald is very much at home in her early 19th century setting.*"

— Jayne Ann Krentz (Amanda Quick) Best-selling Author

"*THIS IS A delightful lighthearted regency frolic.*"

— Genre Go Round Reviews

"*TEA LEAVES AND TAROT CARDS is rich in secondary characters across the spectrum. "TEA LEAVES AND TAROT CARDS has a lot to offer with its original characters and imaginative plot.*"

— Romance Reviews Today

"*IT IS CLEAR that Seewald's goal is to offer a deeply felt, emotional romance.*"

— Library Journal

AUTHOR BIOGRAPHY

Multiple award-winning author, Jacqueline Seewald, has taught creative, expository and technical writing at Rutgers University as well as high school English. She also worked as both an academic librarian and an educational media specialist.

Twenty of her books of fiction have previously been published to critical praise. Her short stories, poems, essays, reviews and articles have appeared in hundreds of diverse publications and numerous anthologies. Jacqueline also has a collection of short stories: BEYOND THE BO TREE: TEN TALES OF ROMANCE.

JACQUELINE SEEWALD

Milton Keynes UK
Ingram Content Group UK Ltd.
UKHW041820300824
447675UK00002B/3